"Hey, Luke, you get new glasses?" David piped.

Alexandra turned at her son's query, a smile ready.

Her smile collapsed. Indeed, she was hard-pressed not to gape at the devastatingly good-looking man approaching. The night of the robbery she'd thought Luke had seemed more relaxed, less rigid, with his jacket off and tie loosened.

But she'd never seen him like this. Surely a new pair of glasses couldn't make so much difference.

His white T-shirt molded his broad shoulders, chest and biceps like a lover's touch. The jeans fitting his trim hips and strong thighs left little of his sexual definition to the imagination.

The man was the epitome of masculinity. Lusty, tempting, virile masculinity.

Alexandra's palms went damp, her breathing, shallow. Mortified, she tried to control her features.

And Luke grinned. Knowingly.

Dear Reader,

This month it's my pleasure to bring you one of the most-requested books we've ever published: *Loving Evangeline* by Linda Howard. This story features Robert Cannon, first seen in her tremendously popular *Duncan's Bride*, and in Evangeline Shaw he meets a woman who is his perfect match—and then some! Don't miss it!

Don't miss the rest of this month's books, either, or you'll end up regretting it. We've also got *A Very Convenient Marriage* by Dallas Schulze, and the next in Marilyn Pappano's "Southern Knights" miniseries, *Regarding Remy*. And then there's *Surrogate Dad* by Marion Smith Collins, as well as *Not His Wife* by Sally Tyler Hayes and *Georgia on My Mind* by Clara Wimberly. In short, a stellar lineup by some of the best authors going, and they're all yours—courtesy of Silhouette Intimate Moments.

Enjoy!

Leslie Wainger
Senior Editor and Editorial Coordinator

Please address questions and book requests to:
Silhouette Reader Service
U.S.: 3010 Walden Ave., P.O. Box 1325, Buffalo, NY 14269
Canadian: P.O. Box 609, Fort Erie, Ont. L2A 5X3

SURROGATE DAD

MARION SMITH COLLINS

Silhouette®
INTIMATE™MOMENTS®
Published by Silhouette Books
America's Publisher of Contemporary Romance

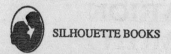 **SILHOUETTE BOOKS**

ISBN 0-373-07610-X

SURROGATE DAD

Copyright © 1994 by Marion Smith Collins

This edition published by arrangement with Harlequin Enterprises B.V.

® and TM are trademarks of Harlequin Enterprises B.V., used under
license. Trademarks indicated with ® are registered in the United States
Patent and Trademark Office, the Canadian Trade Marks Office and in
other countries.

Printed in U.S.A.

Books by Marion Smith Collins

Silhouette Intimate Moments

Another Chance #179
Better Than Ever #252
Catch of the Day #320
Shared Ground #383
Baby Magic #452
Fire on the Mountain #514
Surrogate Dad #610

Silhouette Romance

Home To Stay #773
Every Night at Eight #849

MARION SMITH COLLINS

has written nonfiction for years and is the author of several contemporary romances, as well as one book of general fiction.

She's a devoted traveler and has been to places as far-flung as Rome and Tahiti. Her favorite country for exploring, however, is the United States because, she says, it has everything.

She has been a public relations director, and her love of art inspired her to run a combination gallery and restaurant for several years. In addition, she is a wife and the mother of two children.

She lives with her husband in Georgia.

I would like to thank Bruce Thomas,
who took me to Road Atlanta and introduced me
to the elegant world of vintage racing;
and to our friend, Joe Campbell,
district attorney for the Cherokee Circuit,
who wouldn't let me get away with
anything unethical, even in the name
of poetic license.

This book is dedicated to them and to
my very own personal attorney-at-law, Bob.

Chapter 1

The airport speaker system came to life to announce another flight delay due to strong head winds out over the Atlantic Ocean. The disembodied voice didn't admit to the head winds, of course. A flight from Europe, one from Zambia and another from Bermuda were all delayed because of *weather conditions*.

Alexandra Prescott was meeting her son David's flight, the one from Europe, and she had been here at the Atlanta airport for over an hour. So, along with all the other people who were meeting planes, she'd had plenty of time to hear the questions, the answers and the rumors.

Alexandra's charcoal pencil moved rapidly over the sketch pad in her lap in an attempt to take her mind off her apprehension. At least the international concourse abounded with interesting people.

The sketching was also an attempt to distract herself from other dark thoughts. She hadn't needed the dateline of the morning newspaper to remind her that four years ago today her beloved husband, Daniel, had died, changing her life, and David's, drastically and permanently.

Gradually, as she worked, she became aware of the weight of a gaze. She raised her head, brushed a strand of sand-colored hair behind her ear and glanced around the noisy and crowded airport lounge.

Her attention skimmed over the faces, stopped, backtracked. People shifted, moved, withdrew. She didn't even know what had caught her eye—a subconscious recognition?

She expected to see a smile of greeting or a curious stare, but no one seemed to be paying attention. It was not an unusual occurrence for her to be observed, even approached, when she sketched in a public place.

She never minded being approached; she had encountered any number of interesting and colorful people that way. The children's interest in her drawings was especially gratifying.

But today, not being able to identify the source of the attention left her edgy. She tried to shrug off the annoying feeling and returned to her subject, a tall, elegantly robed Middle-Easterner.

Her pencil slowed. There it was again—the itch across her shoulders that indicated someone was watching.

The fun was gone. She stowed her pad in the large tote bag on the floor by her feet, smoothed her denim skirt and turned her thoughts deliberately to the preparations for her son's homecoming.

"Mrs. Prescott, isn't it?"

She glanced up in surprise at the older man beside her, wondering if he was the source of her unease. His face was vaguely familiar but she couldn't quite place him. He was dressed in designer sweats, spotless athletic shoes and his graying hair looked as if it had just been combed.

He seemed to sense her confusion. "Paul Henderson is my name. West Chadwick introduced us."

West was a neighbor in the condominium complex where she and David lived. But she still didn't—ah, well, she couldn't be rude. "Yes, Mr. Henderson, how are you?" she said, smiling and extending her hand.

At last it came to her. West had invited her to attend a summer party given by his law firm. This man had been there. Was Henderson a client or a lawyer? She couldn't remember.

"May I?" Henderson said, indicating the chair next to her. He was hesitant, but when she nodded he sat down. She became aware of his cologne, something traditional and, if she remembered correctly, very expensive.

"Are you meeting someone?" he asked.

"Yes, I'm meeting my son. He's been visiting his grandparents in Switzerland for the past month. And you, Mr. Henderson?"

"No, I'm saying goodbye, a sadder task." He spoke with all the courtliness and charm of an older generation; and she saw a glitter in his eyes. The lines in his face were deeply scored and intriguing. She wished she dared take out her sketch pad.

At that moment, the arrival of the flight from Switzerland was announced. A surge of relief swept through her. She picked up her tote bag, hooked her arm through the straps and turned to Paul Henderson with a bright smile. "That's my son's flight, Mr. Henderson. Would you excuse me, please? I'm very eager to see him."

He stood politely. "Of course. It's nice to meet you again, Mrs. Prescott."

With the relief singing through her, Alexandra allowed herself to admit that the long delay had worried her. She was aware of the statistics and realized flying was much safer than driving the interstate highways.

Intellectually she knew this, but when her only child was on that plane, her reaction was emotional, not analytical. If anything happened to David—she broke off the unnerving thought.

David had been gone a month, visiting her late husband's parents in Lucerne, and she'd missed him like crazy. She'd missed his company, his quirky logic, his fourteen-year-old antics and even his unbelievable appetite.

She'd prepared his favorite meal for his homecoming—a ghastly, fat-saturated conglomeration of tamales, chili, corn chips, cheese, hamburger and onion. She grimaced. David had an iron stomach, if questionable taste.

She sidestepped a toddler who ricocheted between the rows of seats, stumbled when he reached open space and landed on his well-padded bottom. His mother scooped him up before he could cry, chiding him in beautiful Castilian Spanish.

They exchanged a smile as they both approached the gate where the passengers would disembark.

As Alexandra pulled her station wagon into one of the assigned parking places near the entrance to their home, David became quiet for the first time since they'd left the airport.

His mother glanced over. He was looking toward the dark green front door with the oddest expression on his face. As far as she could tell, there was nothing amiss in the scene. "Something wrong, hon?"

"Not a thing, Mom," he said heartily. Too heartily? "Boy, am I glad to be back."

"Boy, am I glad to have you back," she mimicked. "By the way, I got four Braves tickets for the weekend, right on the first-base line. Okay? You can invite two of your friends."

"Great." He snapped off the seat belt, opened his door and jumped out, flexing his slight body to its full five foot three. "I'm stiff."

David was a bit of a bookworm, but when he was *forced* into inactivity for any length of time he became like a stretched-out rubber band, drawn tight and ready to soar upon release. He had always been slight in build for his age, but she'd begun to notice a change over the summer. This time next year, she'd probably be bemoaning the fact that he was growing too fast.

She watched with a bittersweet smile. She'd hoped the Braves tickets would be more enthusiastically received but she should have known better. He'd have been as happy with the latest book on computers.

She touched the trunk release in the glove compartment. While David dealt with his luggage, she opened the door to the back seat and gathered up the shopping bags he'd been forced to carry onto the plane. Her in-laws always sent David home from these twice-yearly trips laden with gifts.

Had David been a different kind of kid, Alexandra might have tactfully protested their spoiling him. They would have stopped. But so far he seemed unaffected by tangible things.

Besides, he was the Prescotts' only grandchild, and they took a great deal of pleasure in the gift-giving. She wouldn't deny them that pleasure, but she did occasionally wish they'd provide a few practicalities, like underwear and shoes.

In addition to the gifts they bought for him, there were always lavish presents for her—French perfumes and lotions, Swiss chocolates, sometimes bits of delicate crystal from Austria, leather goods from Italy.

"Gramma said to be sure you come with me next Christmas," said David as he hefted his suitcase. "I think they have a man for you to meet."

Alexandra smiled. The idea of her in-laws playing matchmaker amused her. "I don't need another man. I have you."

"Yeah, right." David made a sound somewhere between a snort and a snicker. "Who's that?" he asked.

Alexandra looked over her shoulder to the dark sedan that had just pulled into a nearby space. The condominiums in the medium-size development were clustered in groups of three. She had chosen this complex because of the privacy in each cluster. Their unit, a three-bedroom, was in the center of a U-shaped building, and was flanked by the two smaller units that faced inward. They shared the neatly manicured shrubbery, the tiny scrap of lawn, the flagstone path and broad porch with railing.

"That's a new neighbor. Mr. Quinton...? No, Quinlan. I understand he's building a house and is living in the Lomads's place until it's finished." The neighbors to the right were working in Africa for a year.

Their path converged with the tall man who had gotten out of the car. "Good evening," he said, nodding to Alexandra, glancing curiously at David.

"Good evening." Alexandra started to introduce her son but David spoke before she could.

"Hi," said David, setting down the suitcase and sticking out his hand. "I'm David Prescott. My mom says you're our neighbor."

She held her breath. Lucius Quinlan was such a quiet, formal man, she wasn't sure how he would react to David's spontaneous friendliness.

Lucius shifted his briefcase and shook hands with the youngster, who had a good firm grip. "Yes, I am, for now, anyway. Lucius Quinlan. How do you do, David? Have you been away?"

"Yes, sir. I visit my grandparents every summer for a month. They live in Switzerland."

Lucius nodded. He looked at Alexandra's laden arms. "Do you need any help?"

"No, we're fine," she answered quickly.

He nodded, smiled at David and reached into his pocket for his key. "Nice to meet you, David," he said as he turned away.

"Yes, sir. Nice to meet you, too. Welcome to the neighborhood."

Mom? Luke Quinlan shook his head, incredulous.

He closed the front door behind him, dropped his briefcase on a table. First a cold beer, then a shower, then he would tackle the work he'd brought home. He shed his jacket, and, with a feeling close to relief, yanked at the tie and opened the top button of his shirt.

He took a right turn into the kitchen and grabbed a can of beer from the refrigerator. The gorgeous woman in the adjoining town house was that kid's *mother?*

He halted on his way back to the living room. Instead, he returned to the kitchen, crossed to the bay window and looked out through a crack in the louvered shutters.

He watched as she juggled the packages in her arms while she delved into her big shoulder bag. At last she came up with the key and handed it to the boy.

Even under the burden of the packages, she stood straight as an arrow on those long luscious legs as she waited for David to unlock the door.

Her bearing was one of the first things he'd noticed about her, that and those huge emerald eyes. Her back was straight and she carried her height with self-confidence. She seemed to be comfortable in her body, sure of its capabilities. He shook his head. Still, it was difficult to believe she had a son that age.

Three weeks ago, he'd stood right here in this same spot the first morning after moving in. It had been very early—5:00 a.m.—and still very dark outside. He had just poured a cup of coffee and had gone to the window to check the weather. And stood rooted to the spot.

He grinned to himself at the memory of the lightning-fast shadow. If he'd blinked twice, he'd have missed her. And the spectacular view.

A tousled head of blond hair had poked cautiously through the door. She'd looked around, and, satisfied that no one was watching, had darted barefoot to the edge of the porch to retrieve the morning paper. She had worn a faded T-shirt that barely covered her butt. He'd choked on the coffee.

Since then, it had become an interesting routine. Her sleepwear was diverse, to say the least. One day it was a football jersey; the next a granny gown. The morning she'd come outside in a purple teddy, he'd almost had a heart attack.

A day after the first experience, she had opened her door as he was driving away. He would have been hard-pressed to recognize her. From her early-morning behavior and dress, he had assumed she was young, vivacious. Instead, she was sleekly groomed and sophisticated.

Then there was the day he'd first heard her speak. He'd grown used to southern drawls, some drippy and sweet, some nasal and sulky. Alexandra Prescott's was like honey—deep and elegant, feminine and sexy, and so rich it should have been listed in the Fortune 500.

She was certainly a woman of many contrasts, he thought as he watched Alexandra and her son disappear inside. As Luke turned away, he saw their other neighbor, West Chadwick, pull into his parking space.

Luke grimaced. It was because of West Chadwick that he'd come home with more extra work in his briefcase than usual. The two of them were working together. One of the senior partners in the law firm where they both practiced was transferring his files in preparation for retirement. Luke had an idea that the other seniors in the firm were making this a competition between West Chadwick and himself. That was fine with Luke; he didn't mind competition.

He watched West enter his own condo loaded down with at least as much work as Luke had brought home. The sight left him feeling satisfied.

David came out of his bedroom, whistling. "Something smells good," he announced. His grin turned into a delighted laugh when he saw the dish she had taken from the oven. He reached up to kiss her cheek. "Tamale pie! Mom, you shouldn't have," he said expansively.

"I know. Your arteries are clogged enough." She carried the casserole to the small dining room table and set it on a sturdy iron trivet. David followed with two tall glasses of milk. "I decided homecoming was a special occasion. But you have to eat all the salad, too. Did you finish unpacking?"

"Yep. And put my dirty clothes in the hamper. And stored the suitcase." He spoke with the long-suffering tempo of youth.

She grinned as she pushed his hair out of his eyes and gave him a quick hug. "I'm glad you're home," she said softly.

"Me, too. I needed to be here, especially today." His voice was quiet and choked. "But I think it was hard for Gramma and Grampa to say goodbye to me."

Neither of them had to spell out their feelings on this anniversary of Daniel's death. "I'm sure it was." Alexandra hugged her son again, and this time he held on tight for a long time.

"Daddy would be very proud of you, you know," she whispered.

"He would be proud of you, too," he answered. He finally pulled away, blinking rapidly, and smiled lopsidedly. "After dinner I'm going to install the new microphone Grampa gave me."

That was all the communication they would share for now. It was enough to know that they each had healthy memories, that they could speak of Daniel with ease. The first year or so, it had not been that easy to say his name aloud.

"A microphone?" she asked. Daniel's father loved electronic gadgets and he'd passed the love to David, who was as talented in tinkering as his father and grandfather. She didn't pretend to understand how those things worked, but David understood well enough. "What kind?"

"It's really simple. I just mount it on the wall and I can turn on my computer with my voice. It responds to sound waves."

He kept up the technical description when they sat down and began to eat. Alexandra let him ramble, asking a question occasionally.

When the edge was off David's appetite—and his emotional response under control—he took a long swallow of milk. "The casserole is terrific, Mom. Now, tell me about Mr. Quinlan."

Alexandra shrugged. "I don't know much about him. He's very quiet and very reserved. West—Mr. Chadwick—"

"West?"

She should have known he'd pick up on her use of West Chadwick's first name. She looked at her son. "I went out to dinner with Mr. Chadwick a few times while you were gone. Does that bother you?"

He dug his fork into his salad and avoided her eyes. "I don't like him."

She knew that; he'd made his feelings clear, almost too clear. On occasion she'd had to warn him to keep his remarks to himself. But she wasn't sure of the reason for his dislike—David had always been friendly and outgoing to everyone—unless it was because he thought West was attracted to her.

She had not dated since Daniel's death. Not only did she still feel frozen inside, but there had not been time for men. It was inevitable that David was going to feel some disillusionment when she began.

"Honey," she said gently, then hesitated. How to handle this? If she told him she'd been lonely while he was away, he would become protective and refuse to leave her again. On the other hand, he needed his own interests and so did she.

Teenage boys were so complicated, she thought with a silent sigh. In the end she opted for a coward's way out. "We just went to dinner. I have no intention of getting serious or remarrying—"

"Well, you should remarry. You're a young woman. I'm going off to school in four years and then you'll be all alone."

Alexandra hid her surprise. They had never discussed this subject, but she'd assumed it would be a touchy one. Suddenly the light dawned. Her in-laws had a man for her to meet. They must have had a lot to say to David during his visit.

"I want you to date, Mom. I just don't think Mr. Chadwick is the man for you. He's too...too slick, too smooth." David forked another bite of salad into his mouth and chewed contentedly.

She raised an eyebrow.

He swallowed and waved his fork, dismissing West. "You were telling me about Mr. Quinlan."

Alexandra shook her head, trying to pick up the thread of the conversation. "He and Mr. Chadwick are friends and practice law together at the same downtown firm," she said. "That's how Mr. Quinlan knew the condo was available on a temporary basis." She poured cream into her coffee and stirred absently. "David—"

"Mr. Quinlan had a gleam in his eye when he looked at you, Mom. I think he likes you." He grinned with a pseudosophisticated look in his eyes.

If she was surprised before, she was stunned now. A hoot of laughter escaped and she tried to disguise it with a cough. She put her napkin to her mouth.

An image of Lucius Quinlan rose in her mind. Horn-rimmed glasses, wing-tipped shoes, dark, conservative suits and a very serious demeanor. "A gleam in his eye? Honey, Mr. Quinlan is a very nice man, but he's very quiet, very formal. I seriously doubt anything as frivolous as a gleam would appear in his eye."

David shook his head, smiling patiently as though she didn't know what she was talking about. "I don't think he's so bad. At least he's not slick."

She had to agree with him there. Lucius Quinlan was definitely not slick. And he wasn't really bad-looking, or wouldn't be if he'd just loosen up a bit.

Controlled was a word she associated with him. He was...rigid. He rarely smiled and even when he did, it was a controlled smile. He was tall, but it was hard to judge his body type under the Brooks Brothers sack suits he wore. And his glasses had such heavy frames that his eyes were practically invisible.

However, there was something about the man that made her wary, something about him that didn't quite ring true. She forced her thoughts away from Lucius Quinlan.

"Dessert?" she asked brightly as she rose with her plate in her hand.

"I'm not through with my salad yet," David said, looking puzzled.

During the rest of the meal, Alexandra deliberately kept the conversation and her questions on his grandparents and his visit. As soon as they'd finished, he went to his room to tinker.

A few hours later, Alexandra was propped up against her pillows, making a list of all the things that had to be done to get her son ready for the new school year.

She'd urged David to go to bed soon after dinner in an attempt to get his system adjusted to the change in time zones. He'd gone, but she could still hear the rhythm of drumbeats from his stereo.

She was half listening to the eleven o'clock news, coming from the small television set in the corner. And thinking about her son's observations of Lucius Quinlan.

She laughed under her breath. A gleam in his eye? That stuffy man? Never. She shrugged away the thought and returned to compiling her list.

Shoes were first on it. She hoped, without much confidence, that he wouldn't want those hundred-dollar jobs all his friends were wearing, but this was his first year of high school—a milestone.... She tapped the pencil against her lip and stared at the flickering tube. Maybe she could find a discount outlet.

Suddenly her gaze narrowed on the set. She gasped and grabbed the remote control. She fumbled to increase the volume, sending it blasting through the room before she finally got it under control.

"My God," she breathed.

"Captain Brigadol's body was found in the parking lot reserved for airport employees," said the reporter. "Police suspect the murder is a possible link to a smuggling operation they have been investigating."

"My God," she exclaimed. She threw back the covers and leapt across the floor to where she'd dropped her purse. She picked it up and extracted her sketch pad. The sketch of the man was near the front of the book, one of the first she'd done that afternoon.

She stared at the handsome face, the tailored uniform, feeling sick. A few hours ago he had been alive. No, more than alive, she thought as she looked at his compelling smile. A few hours ago she had seen him, sketched him. Suddenly, she was horrified at the realization of how quickly a life could be snuffed out.

"Mom? What's going on? I thought I heard you yell."

She stared at her son.

"Are you all right?"

She shook her head and squeezed her eyes shut. "Yes, I'm all right. It was just on the news. A man I saw today while I was waiting for your plane—he was murdered."

He climbed onto the bed and hugged her. The clumsily protective gesture made her smile, but she appreciated the effort. "Gee, Mom. That's awful. Did you know him?" He gestured to the sketch pad in her lap. "Is that his picture?"

"No, I didn't know him. I was just drawing people in the crowd while I waited for your plane."

Horror stories on the nightly news had become commonplace, statistics that were horrifying to her but rarely within personal reach. She feared becoming desensitized like a lot of other Americans. Even worse, she feared her son's becoming desensitized.

But this man, this pilot's face was one she would never forget. She felt connected to him, if only through her drawing. For a brief moment in time their paths had crossed, and now he was dead.

David's expression was worried. She touched his hand where it rested on her shoulder. "I'm fine, David. Really, I am. Go back to bed."

"You sure?"

"I'm sure. See you in the morning."

"Okay." He left. And she noted automatically that he was outgrowing his pajamas, too, that they would have to be added to the list.

She leafed through the other drawings in her book. She had drawn the sailor and the salesman, the priest and the spinster, the harried mother and the haute couture model.

Children especially delighted her. Their grubby fingers and tousled hair, the gaps in their grins, and best of all, the open, frank way they had of studying the people around them. Their faces were easy and amusing to draw.

The images progressed from her keen eye to a recognizable likeness on the page with a minimum number of lines. Indeed, the people she sketched were identifiable more by attitude and bearing and some small, original characteristic that made them unique, than by a realistic portrayal of any one face.

Alexandra didn't think of herself as an artist; she was a caricaturist. And she did it very well.

Daniel's death in a plane crash had altered overnight what was to have been a comfortable, if predictable, suburban life, altered it to a solitary struggle.

The grief had been staggering, the first months a nightmare. She'd had to learn to function totally alone, while at the same time fighting to keep the despair and disruption of her son's life to a minimum.

She'd won some of the battles and lost some, she decided. Daniel would have had suggestions for improvement, of course, but he wouldn't have been profoundly disappointed in her.

She returned to the picture of the pilot. *I'm so sorry,* she said to the man, touching his smiling image with her fingertips. She would find out if he was married and had children. If so, maybe his family would like to have the drawing.

Smuggling, the newscaster had said. Did he mean the pilot had been suspected of smuggling? She briefly considered calling the police.

What for? What would she say? She'd drawn a picture of the man they'd found murdered this afternoon? They'd think she was certifiable.

Chapter 2

Friday morning, Alexandra was washing dishes when she heard David talking animatedly to someone outside on the porch. Curious, she picked up a towel to dry her hands and went to the window.

It was Lucius Quinlan. Dressed for work in his customary dark suit and conservative tie, he stood, briefcase in one hand, keys in the other, listening to David. From this angle, and in contrast to David, Lucius appeared much taller than she'd thought he was.

As she watched, he tossed the keys and caught them several times. The activity might have been a sign of impatience, she couldn't tell, but she stood ready to intervene.

Finally, he nodded and said something that brought color and an embarrassed grin to David's face. Then he headed down the flagstone path toward his car. He raised his hand in casual salute to the boy as he drove off.

David waved back, seemingly unconcerned, then stood looking after the car until it rounded the bend and disappeared. The set of his shoulders seemed tight, somehow almost defensive.

Alexandra snapped the towel over her shoulder. On impulse she knocked on the window. If that man had said something to hurt or embarrass David, she would give him a piece of her mind.

David hesitated for a heartbeat. Then he turned, grinning, and gave her a thumbs-up. She felt her tension ease.

The Braves won. The game was a high-scoring, hit-and-run, four-pitcher, screamingly wild rout. They were on their feet almost as much as they were in their seats.

It was exactly what Alexandra had needed to chase away a blue mood. Her sadness at the news of the pilot's death had lingered for the past two days. She had not been able to get the man's face out of her mind.

When she, David and his two friends had arrived at their seats in the stadium, David's friend Bill had come out with one of those silly, teenage kinds of questions. "Those seats are great, Mrs. Prescott. Who did you have to kill to get us right behind the dugout?"

At any other time, the comment would not have even registered. But at his words, the pilot's features had floated across her vision. She had attempted to shrug off the boy's comment. "One of the players' wives, who bought a sketch of mine at Christmas, called the art shop last week, Bill," she said. "She wanted a present for her husband's birthday. We swapped."

"Mr. Quinlan told me this morning that this series is sold out," David said importantly. "He tried to get tickets, too, but he couldn't. He said I was lucky to have such a resourceful mother."

So that was what the conversation had been about. "And don't you forget it, buddy." She tugged affectionately at the bill of his Braves cap. She wore one, as well. He'd insisted that she get one for herself, too, when she'd stopped outside the stadium to buy hats for all three boys. He'd given her a very adult grin when she'd put it on. "Lookin' good, Mom."

She dropped the boys at their homes and was assured that she had their undying gratitude. "If you ever need anything, Mrs. Prescott, I'm your man," said Eddie, a freckle-faced urchin with eyes like dark chocolate. "Anything."

"Thank you, Eddie. I'll keep that in mind."

"Why don't we stop for dogs at the Varsity?" David asked when they were alone. "We could take them home and save you from having to cook supper." The sun was gone but darkness hadn't yet settled on the city. The heat was still heavy in the air.

"How thoughtful of you to suggest it," she answered with a wry chuckle. The Varsity drive-in, near the Georgia Tech campus, had a colorful history and a reputation for the best chili dogs in the country.

She glanced at him, noting that his nose and cheeks were red. She felt a twinge of guilt because she hadn't thought to bring sunscreen. A smear of catsup on his

wrinkled T-shirt bore witness to the hamburger he'd
had at the game. She should insist on vegetables for
dinner, but he'd told her more than once that she had
to stop treating him like a kid.

Sometimes she feared her own inadequacy. She tried
hard to be a good mother, to see that David had the
right kinds of foods, to keep close tabs on his school-
work, to include his friends in their lives. As he ma-
tured, she had been careful to give him more freedom.
So far, he had abided by the responsibility that went
along with it.

Unfortunately, her purchase of the caps hadn't kept
the sun off any of their faces. She could feel the sting
of her own skin and wondered if her nose was as red
as David's.

*Ah, well, the damage will not be permanent and I
am not going to worry about it today. Today is for fun.*

She sighed. "Okay, the Varsity it is."

When school started, their free time would be
sharply curbed, defined by David's homework and
school activities and her own erratic schedule. Occasionally she wondered if she wouldn't have been better off going to a job with regular nine-to-five hours.

Sometimes she had days, even weeks without a major sale. Then she would receive a special order and
have to work nonstop until it was filled. She loved the
way she worked but it wasn't routine. And, though she
was coping, it certainly wasn't financially secure, either.

Recently she'd been approached by a local ad
agency to go to work for them full-time. The job

would mean predictable hours. She preferred drawing spontaneously. But maybe she should try it.

The mouth-watering smell of chili dogs and french fries filled the car. Alexandra braked to let a dark van turn left out of the complex before she drove through the gates. She continued around the well-lighted ellipse to park in front of their building.

"I'll get the food—you unlock the door," David offered.

"Okay." She unlocked the door. Leaving the key ring dangling, she reached inside to flip the light switch, and stood back to let David precede her. She paused to retrieve her keys.

"Uh, Mom..." David had stopped just over the threshold in the small entrance hall. The two bags with their distinctive red-and-gold Varsity logo dropped at his feet.

"David, be careful," she scolded. "You'll spill..." Her voice trailed off as she saw what had prompted his mishap. "Oh, my God," she whispered.

The room beyond was a wreck. Chairs overturned, picture frames lying in pools of broken glass, empty spaces in the bookshelves where television and stereo had been.

David started to move forward.

"No!" Alexandra grabbed his shirt and began to back up. "Come on," she whispered.

"But my room. I have to—" David began in a normal voice.

She shushed him as she pulled him out and closed the door behind them. "Someone may still be inside."

"Mom, if anyone were there, they would have heard us by now."

Nonetheless, she kept a hold on her son as she headed for West Chadwick's condo. The lights were on; she rang the bell. *Hurry, hurry,* she chanted silently to herself, watching over her shoulder, ready to scream bloody murder, if necessary.

West opened the door, dressed in shorts, a towel slung around his neck. "Alexandra. What a pleasant surprise. Hello, David."

Without waiting for an invitation, Alexandra pulled her son through the door and slammed it behind her. "Call the police!"

"What?"

"Call the police!" she demanded, her voice rising. She realized her body was shaking. "I've been robbed. The condo—"

David stepped in at that moment. "We just got home," he told West calmly. "Someone has trashed our place. May we use your phone?"

Her son was more composed than she was, thought Alexandra. "Yes, yes. Please." Her hands fluttered uselessly through the air.

West had not waited to hear more. He was already at the phone, punching in 911. He gave the operator the details. "Have a seat," he said to the two of them when he'd hung up. "I'll get dressed."

They waited in the living room. Alexandra's fears had calmed and the inevitable concerns were beginning to crowd her mind. How had the thieves gotten past the guard at the entrance to the complex? And how had they gotten inside her condo? The door had still been locked.

She sat gingerly on the edge of a chair while David roamed around the room. Beyond the hallway, a sliver of another room, intended as a den or a second bedroom, was visible. In their condo, the room served as a studio for Alexandra, but West had set it up as a weight room.

"He's a bodybuilder." David said the words with a tinge of scorn.

"An exercise freak," West corrected as he joined them, buttoning his shirt. He viewed David with a lifted eyebrow but didn't comment on the sarcasm. "Sitting behind a desk all day rusts the joints. You're welcome to try out the equipment sometime, David."

The boy turned away. "No, thanks," he muttered.

His voice bordered on insolence. Alexandra opened her mouth to berate him for his manners when suddenly the sound of sirens reached their ears. She settled for a glare and they all went outside to meet the police.

And Lucius Quinlan. He burst through his door, looking ready to do battle. He still wore his suit trousers and dress shirt. But his tie was missing, his shirt open at the collar, his sleeves turned back. In the light from the revolving blue bubble atop the police car, which reflected from the lenses of his glasses, he looked dangerous. "What's going on?"

David headed across the porch and answered for them. "Hey, Mr. Quinlan, guess what? Someone broke in while Mom and me were at the ball game." He joined the first policeman who had hurried up.

"Mister, I need to check on my room. I've got some important stuff in there!"

"Stand back, son." The man hadn't drawn his gun, but he looked ready to.

Alexandra caught David's arm. "We will check everything, David. As soon as the police say it's all right."

He turned back to Luke. "Our place is really trashed. You should see—"

"David!" Alexandra remonstrated. She realized that he was beginning to relish this situation with too much adolescent glee.

Two more uniformed officers had arrived; they approached her. Another patrol car pulled in. A couple of neighbors, out for a walk, wandered over.

The porch seemed crowded, too crowded. The whirling blue lights distorted faces, turning them into unearthly masks. Alexandra had trouble getting her breath. Despite the late-summer weather, she suddenly felt chilled.

Questions were coming at her from all sides. At the same time, she was trying to keep track of David, who was arguing with the first policeman about the sacks from the Varsity.

Of all people, it was Lucius who interpreted her frantic look correctly. He made his way to her side. "Why don't I take David to my place while you talk to the police?" he said quietly.

She gave him a distracted glance. "Are you sure you wouldn't mind? I don't know how long it will take."

One of the police officers called to her. Still she hesitated.

"Go," Lucius said. "David will be fine."

"Did you see anything? Anyone hanging around?" West asked Lucius.

"No. You?"

"Not a thing," West said. "I'll take care of explaining to the neighbors. I guess the cops will want to talk to everyone." He went to a group standing near the porch and steered them away from the scene.

Lucius nodded, his hand at Alexandra's back, urging her toward her door. "Thank you," she said over her shoulder. "If you can get the police to release the evidence, those sacks have his supper in them." She pointed to the sacks that someone had moved to a table beside the front door.

"I'll convince them."

"Mrs. Prescott, I'm Sergeant Pendleton. Please come this way."

As she followed the sergeant into the condo, she dodged a woman who was examining the doorframe. Another man worked on the bookshelves. "There are scratches around the front-door lock. I'd suggest you get a locksmith here as soon as possible."

"Yes, of course. Do you know any that work at night?"

"Several do. It would be a good idea to have him install a dead bolt, too."

"I'll call immediately."

Sergeant Pendleton gave her an approving nod. "Just a few questions first. You had to unlock the door when you and the boy arrived?"

"Yes."

"So the thieves—we think there were two—must have broken in, locked the door while they worked and left from the back. That door is unlocked. I've sent a man to talk to the people around the swimming pool."

All of the buildings in the complex were built facing the elliptical road, leaving the large area behind the units as a communal park. "There's a picnic area back there, too, and cookout grills," she said.

"One of my men will canvas the complex and question the guard at the gate. If there is a witness, we'll find him." He took her arm to keep her from stepping on broken glass. "Aside from the television and stereo, do you see anything missing in the living room?"

She looked at the man blankly. "How can I possibly tell until this mess is cleaned up?"

"A quick walk-through will do for now. We can always add to the inventory later, but the sooner we get the word out on what we do know, the better the chance we have of recovering your goods."

Alexandra knew the odds for recovery were almost nil. And to be honest, she didn't care. Things could be replaced. She was just glad that she and David hadn't been at home when the burglars broke in. Or worse, walked in on them. "Okay," she agreed.

Something was odd, she thought as she made her way through the rooms. Decidedly odd. The pillows were tossed, the plants lay on their sides, spilling dirt, the covers were off the beds, but nothing was torn or leaking feathers or destroyed. Except for some scattered potting soil and the broken glass from a couple of framed prints, everything was whole. Pick things up off the floor, run the vacuum cleaner, and it would look the same as before, except for the missing TV and stereo.

"It seems curious that my jewelry is still here, and they left this small TV," she told the officer when they were looking around her bedroom. "Don't you think so, Sergeant?"

He shrugged. "Most thieves are not known for their intelligence."

In David's room the mattress had been pulled off the bed, the desk chair lay on its side. Nothing seemed to be missing but, of course, David would have to verify that, himself. She moved on to the studio.

And gasped at the mess. This room was the worst affected. Paint had been spilled, charcoal ground into the floor, her drawing board overturned.

Then she saw the gap on the shelves. "My sketchbooks are gone," she said, stunned. "Why on earth would anyone steal sketchbooks?"

"I don't know," said the sergeant. He sounded as though he didn't care, either. But, she saw, he was crouching beside a painted chest she used for storage. What had caught his eye was a partial handprint clearly outlined in charcoal.

Even to the uninitiated, the distinctive pattern of lines and whorls showed up vividly against the ivory enamel. He called out to one of his men, his voice showing the first trace of enthusiasm.

Alexandra left them to it.

"As soon as they're finished here, I'll help you clean up," said West a short time later. They were sitting on the sofa, watching people come and go. The air-conditioning was going right along with them, out the door, to be replaced by August heat and humidity. Alexandra fanned herself with a magazine.

At last the police informed Alexandra that they had finished. She went to the door with Sergeant Pendleton, the last to go. She was relieved. From the sternness of some of their questions, you would have thought *she* was the suspect.

Another officer awaited the sergeant outside. They conferred for a minute. Then they left together on foot.

She wanted nothing as much as she wanted to take a cool bath and crawl into bed. But in spite of her exhaustion, she called the locksmith. He promised to be there in an hour.

West had helped her right the furniture and pick up the worst of the mess. She finally got rid of him, too.

She noticed, as she was going to knock on Lucius's door, that one police car remained at the curb. Sergeant Pendleton stood beside it, talking to another man.

"Mrs. Prescott, one more question, please." He loped toward her. "Did you happen to notice any strange cars around the complex when you came home tonight?" he asked when he reached the porch.

"No—wait. Yes, I saw a van."

"When? Where?"

"It was pulling out of the gates as we returned from the ball game. I didn't pay any attention at the time. There are less than a hundred units here and you learn to recognize the cars. But anyone could have bought a new van."

"It was new?"

"I had the impression that it was. I'm not familiar with models."

"Do you remember the color?"

She thought carefully. "Dark. Navy blue or black, I think. Why? Did someone else see something?"

"The guard says a van left the complex a short time before we were called. The vehicle drove out without stopping. It may belong to one of the owners. We haven't checked with everyone yet.

"But the guard insists that he never saw it enter through the gates." He shrugged. "That may or may not check out. And the van did not have a parking authorization sticker on the bumper."

Her eyes grew round. "Then if it was them, and if we had been a few minutes earlier, we could have walked in while they were robbing us."

The statement was so obvious, even to her own ears, that he didn't bother to answer. "Did you call the locksmith?" he asked her quietly.

"Yes, I did. He'll be here in about an hour."

"Good. Well—good night, Mrs. Prescott. I'm afraid this is another random robbery, and our chances of catching the guys who did it are pretty slim. However, there is that partial palm print we found in your studio. Anyway, we'll call you as soon as we have anything."

"Good night, Sergeant," she said numbly. After a minute, she walked to Lucius's door and knocked.

"It's open."

She cracked the door and leaned in. The entrance hall was dark but there were lights in the room beyond. "David?" she called as she stepped over the threshold.

"He's in the living room," said a deep voice from beside her.

Alexandra whirled, startled suddenly by a large shape looming out of the darkness of the kitchen. Her hand went to her breast.

"Sorry," said Lucius. He didn't sound sorry. He sounded amused. Damn him. After all she'd been through tonight, she didn't care to be the object of his amusement. She looked more closely.

This was not the Lucius Quinlan she was accustomed to seeing. What on earth had he done to himself? The glasses were missing. One dark eyebrow arched provocatively. Seen from this angle, his shoulders seemed so broad. So... so... broad!

"Mom? Is that you?"

"Yes, it's me," she answered rather uneasily.

"Guess what, Mom?" David said. He appeared at the living room entrance. His excitement raised his voice a full octave as he hurried toward her. "Luke has a vintage race car."

She moved forward into the light to meet her son. When she glanced back at the man behind her, he had replaced his glasses and his expression had returned to the bland, noncommittal detachment she'd expected. Embarrassed at her overreaction, she concluded that her impression must have been a trick of the shadows.

"What's a vintage race car?" she asked absently, touching the boy's shoulder.

David was holding a large coffee-table book. "Any race car that's over a certain age. Luke has some extra tickets for the Labor Day races at Road Atlanta and he's offered them to us. Can we go?"

She stared at her son, hearing nothing but the sergeant's words. What would have happened if they had walked in on the thieves? She shuddered, thinking that David could have been in terrible danger. He could have been attacked, beaten, murdered.

He was her son; she was responsible for his safety and well-being. Her anxiety built. And her fear.

He seemed to be okay. She had worried that he might be troubled and uneasy, but she was grateful now to see a smile. Clearly, Lucius had found a diversion to take David's mind off the break-in.

Her son was giving her an impatient look. What had he asked . . . ?

"Didn't you hear me? Luke has—"

"Mr. Quinlan," she corrected automatically. "Car races?"

"Your mother has other things on her mind, David. We can discuss this later."

David was immediately contrite. "I'm sorry, Mom. Are you okay?"

She slanted Luke an appreciative look. "I'm fine, honey. Just shaken a bit."

"Why don't you sit down?" Lucius asked her. "I have a fresh pot of coffee. Would you like some?"

She hesitated. "I've called a locksmith." Then she changed her mind. The air-conditioning felt like heaven. "But he won't be here for a while yet." She sat on the sofa. "Thank you. I'd love a cup of coffee. Black, please."

He disappeared into the shadows again. David came to sit beside her and opened the large book on his lap. "See this, Mom?" He swiveled the book so that she could see the colorful photograph of a sleek, red race car, a car of another day, another age. It was distinctive because of its difference. "This is like the car Luke races. Well, sorta like it. His is silver."

"Honey, you should call him Mr. Quinlan." Race cars? Lucius Quinlan was a racer?

"I asked David to call me Luke. And I hope you will, too."

She nodded. Lucius—Luke, she corrected herself—had come back into the room silently. She noticed for the first time that he was in his stocking feet. The fact startled her almost as much as finding that he raced vintage race cars.

He set the cup of coffee, along with a snifter, on a small table beside her. From a decanter he poured a scant inch in the bottom of the crystal glass. "Have some of this first. I'm afraid David finished the hot dogs," he said, glancing at the empty cups and papers on the coffee table. "Would you like something to eat?"

"No, thank you. I'm not hungry." She frowned at her son. "David, you know better than to leave a mess like this."

"Sorry," he said with a sheepish grin. He started to gather up the wrappings and stuff them into the sacks. "I'll throw them away."

"Trash can's under the sink," Luke told him.

She took a sip of the fine brandy. The liquid slipped down her throat, warming her as the aromatic fumes reached her nose. She felt some of the tension seep from her muscles. She sighed and set the glass aside. The coffee was fresh and hot, the aroma more pleasing than that of the liqueur. "That's very good. Do you have children of your own, Luke?"

Luke was momentarily taken aback by the question. He was seldom at a loss, and he was not sure why, on this occasion, he should have been. He was the right age to be a father. "No, I've never been married."

"Oh. I thought—you seem to relate well to kids."

She was trying to make conversation, trying to get her mind off what had happened. Her hands trembled slightly as she grasped the cup. It was the first sign of vulnerability she'd ever shown in his presence.

He felt an unexpected wave of sympathy. "I like David," he said, surprised to realize that he meant it.

"So do I." She smiled, activating a dimple he hadn't noticed before.

In the silence that followed her words, Luke studied her—her white walking shorts and matching shirt, the baseball cap tipped back on her head, the sunburned nose—and decided that he liked her, too. Wearing that getup, she could have been the very young woman he'd first thought her to be.

David came back into the room and plopped down in a chair, looking very much at home. "You look tired, Mom," he said.

"I've never been burglarized before," she answered ruefully. "It takes something out of you." She hesitated. "David, when we came back from the ball game, did you notice a van you didn't recognize?"

He thought for a minute. "Yeah, I did. Coming out just as we started to turn through the gates of the complex. Do the police think the van belonged to the thieves?"

"They're not certain. Maybe."

"Did the police find anything else significant?" Luke asked her.

She tilted her head to one side, pondering before she answered. "I'm not sure," she said slowly, speculatively. "They don't seem to consider it significant, but I was surprised that the thieves didn't touch my jewelry. Or the television in my bedroom. On the other hand, they took my sketch pads, which have no value at all."

Luke was baffled, too. Why would anyone take her drawings? They certainly couldn't sell them; her work was too well-known.

"It seems odd to me but the police didn't seem to feel it was important." She sipped from her cup.

"Maybe they just liked the way you draw," David said. "I need to check on my room," he added, showing signs of impatience. Luke's efforts to distract him were apparently losing their effectiveness.

Alexandra couldn't quite squelch a soft groan as she set down the coffee cup and forced herself to her feet. She felt achy; she hoped she wasn't coming down with something. A summer cold, maybe? "Yes. And I have to be there for the locksmith."

When they reached the door of her condo, David turned to address Luke. "'Night, Luke. Thanks for letting me look at your racing books."

"You're welcome, David. We'll talk about the races later. Good night."

David disappeared. Standing at the door, Alexandra looked at Luke. "I want to thank you again for keeping him occupied tonight. It was a big help."

"I enjoyed having him," Luke said absently, as he followed her to the porch. For a reason he didn't fully understand, he was reluctant to let her go inside. He wanted to keep her talking, at least for a while. "Do you need help cleaning up?"

"West helped me. We picked up the pillows and straightened the furniture. The rest can wait until morning."

"Of course," he said sarcastically.

That brought her head up. Her eyebrows came together over those gorgeous green eyes. Clearly, she didn't like his tone but she let it pass.

He decided he didn't care for the tone much, either. He was letting his dislike for West Chadwick color his attitude, but she needn't be a target of his mockery. Certainly not tonight.

"You know, as we were straightening the rooms, something else seemed peculiar," she added thoughtfully as she crossed to the decorative wrought-iron barrier at the edge of the porch and wrapped her hands around the top rail. "At first glance the place seemed to have been vandalized, but nothing was actually destroyed." She seemed to be talking to herself. "The worst of the damage was in my studio.

That's what doesn't make sense. One glance could have told the burglar that there was nothing of value in there. And why would they take old sketchbooks? Almost as though they didn't like me personally.''

Luke looked at her hands, white-knuckled, curled around the rail and knew a sudden urge to cover them with his own. "Who have you satirized lately?" he asked dryly.

She turned, crossing her arms, and frowned at him. He hid a smile, noting that she was visibly irritated, a condition alien to her usual air of smooth refinement. "You know what I do?" she asked coolly.

She drew very perceptive caricatures. Some of them were generic figures. He'd seen a row of them—illustrating stereotypical players in the dating game—on the wall of a popular restaurant for singles in Buckhead.

But others depicted well-known Atlanta personalities. Politicians, sports figures, people in the entertainment fields, they all came under her good-natured, but occasionally penetrating, scrutiny. "Sure. I've seen your drawings in the shops around town. You're good."

She relaxed slightly, leaned one slender hip against the railing. "Then you should know that my caricatures aren't malicious," she told him.

"No, they are not malicious, just keenly perceptive." He shoved his hands into the pockets of his trousers and looked at her. "You frequently reveal an insight that probably makes your subjects uncomfortable." He tried a smile, which was ignored.

He'd meant the comment as a sincere compliment but it didn't seem to pacify her. He turned his head just enough to meet her eyes. "They are funny," he added.

When he'd first seen her name on a caricature, he'd been amazed. An elegant woman like Alexandra Prescott would surely lack the sense of the absurd revealed in the drawings. He knew she had been widowed for several years; maybe this was the only way she *could* reveal her sense of humor.

"You think maybe someone did this because he or she doesn't like being laughed at?" She straightened, began to pace in short bursts of energy. "Do you?" she demanded, stopping abruptly, feet apart.

He frowned, took a step toward her as though to comfort her. Stopped. The movement had put his face in shadow. "Hell, I don't know," he said finally, with an explosive sigh.

Her voice climbed the scale with each word. "I don't know, either, but I tell you, it makes me damned mad that someone could enter a patrolled complex, and brazenly—" she waved her hand "— break into another person's home. All for a TV and stereo that are almost as old as David." She planted her fists on her trim hips. She was breathing fast, like a runner at the end of the Peachtree Road Race. "Why? Tell me that. Why?"

Luke's heartbeat accelerated as he stared at her, suddenly realizing that this woman was not merely angry, she was mad as hell. And she was magnificent. This emotion was totally different from the little bout of irritation she'd shown when she thought he was criticizing her drawings.

No, this was passionate anger, and she was glorious in its throes. Beneath the shadowing bill of the baseball cap, her emerald eyes flashed like hot lightning. Her chin rose to a dangerous angle, and a muscle in her jaw pulsated. Luke caught himself before he laughed in admiration.

Her fear and vulnerability had dissolved totally, swept away by the healing wind of outrage. He wasn't a psychiatrist but he would imagine the evolution was normal, and the angry emotion, healthier.

She came to a halt near her door and stood glaring as though she could see through the wood. "Why?" she repeated after a moment. Her breathing had slowed and she was speaking at her normal level now.

"What motivates any criminal nowadays?" Luke said, then he stopped.

Her anger had been spent. He didn't want her to become depressed again. When he spoke again, his attitude was practical, realistic. "I think you and David were lucky not to have been at home." He went on, hoping to add calm to the equation, "Your delay at the Varsity might have prevented a dangerous confrontation."

"I realize that." She shuddered. When he saw her slender shoulders move, he felt a qualm. He hoped he hadn't reintroduced her fears.

She seemed okay. "I still feel that taking the sketchbooks was an odd thing to do. And I'll probably never know why." She straightened. "Well, I guess

I'd better go in. Thank you again for entertaining David and for the coffee.''

"Would you like to have dinner some night?" Luke asked out of the blue.

Suddenly, he sensed genuine withdrawal. "You're very kind, but I don't date," she said formally.

Which was a damned lie, Luke thought, annoyed as he watched her disappear into her condo. She'd gone out with West Chadwick twice that he knew of.

Why had she lied? Alexandra asked herself angrily. She *never* lied. He'd probably seen her leaving for dinner with West.

Why the hell had he even asked? Luke wondered. Of course, he knew the answer. The feeling of warmth he experienced when she blinked her heavy lashes and turned those emerald eyes on him. And simple lust, arising from those early-morning glimpses of long legs, full breasts, mussed hair and that damned purple teddy.

Since they were both early risers, he'd gotten into the habit of checking at the window each morning, like some crazy Tom, peeping out instead of in. He would break that habit beginning tomorrow.

He could dismiss Alexandra Prescott easily from his mind. She wasn't even his type. He liked women who smiled a lot, who were warm and passionate, who weren't afraid to demonstrate a bit of feminine vulnerability.

Alexandra was more West's type. Tall, coolly elegant, a thoroughbred to her toes. In control—of her responses, of her emotions, of her life. She was the kind of woman the other lawyer always dated.

Alexandra reentered her studio with a sense of consternation. She sincerely regretted her quick response. Luke had been very nice tonight, a bit more relaxed than she'd ever seen him, and she'd cut him off tactlessly.

Still, there was something about Lucius Quinlan that bothered her. Something not quite defined. She knew nothing about him except that he was a lawyer; he was building a house; he raced cars for a hobby.

But that something stood like a ghostly presence at his shoulder.

Chapter 3

"Mr. Quinlan? Mr. Chadwick would like a moment of your time if it is convenient." The voice on the telephone had all the warmth of a robotic recording.

Luke didn't like Chadwick's secretary any more than he liked the man himself. In the constant corporate battle of who was more important than whom, the woman was a general on the front lines. Ordinarily he would treat such a summons with amusement, but for some reason her attitude annoyed him today.

"When?" he asked, wondering why the hell the man didn't just call himself.

"As soon as possible."

"Fine. I'm free now. Tell him to come right over."

He hung up before the woman could suggest that *he* come to *her* employer's office. He buzzed his own secretary and told her to show Mr. Chadwick in as soon as he arrived. He took off his glasses and rubbed the bridge of his nose.

Chadwick arrived, grim-faced and agitated. "How much do you know about setting up offshore corporations?" he asked as soon as he was seated across from Luke.

"Not a hell of a lot," Luke answered warily, reseating his glasses.

"Neither do I," West said.

Luke almost smiled at the other lawyer's woeful expression. Almost, but not quite. The rivalry between himself and West Chadwick, encouraged by the senior partners in order to up the billable hours, had been going on for months. Hell, years!

On more than one occasion, the competition had reached a bitter level. He and Chadwick were very different, socially, intellectually, personally. In other circumstances, he supposed, they would have complemented each other. Instead, they had grown into wholehearted adversaries.

But lately to Luke, the struggle hadn't seemed worth the bad taste it left in his mouth. He wasn't sure quite yet what steps he would take. He was in pretty good shape financially for the first time in his life. He wouldn't jeopardize that, but the situation was going to change. "What's up?" he asked.

"Our client has decided to move his manufacturing operation to the Caribbean."

"What?" Luke leaned forward, his forearms on the desk. He picked up a pencil. "Why the devil would he do that?"

"I asked. I was told it was none of my business." Chadwick shook his head. "That's a hell of a thing to say to your lawyer."

"Does Bolton know?" Luke asked, naming the retiring partner from whom they had taken over the client.

"I don't think so. Look, Quinlan, I know we don't get along all that well, but we need to tread carefully on this one."

"I agree." Luke's eyebrows drew together. "Is he moving his family to the Caribbean?"

"Apparently." Chadwick propped his elbows on the arms of his chair and tented his fingers. "The man is on every charity board in town. He's always seemed very protective of his social and community image. This doesn't make sense, Luke."

It was the first time Chadwick had ever used Luke's given name. Though he was amazed and curious, Luke subdued an impulse to react. "It makes me downright suspicious. I don't care if he is our client."

Chadwick opened his mouth, then closed it again and shrugged. "Anyway, we may run into some other problems. His company makes some of the computer chips for the defense department, doesn't it?"

Luke cursed. "So we'll have the government looking over our shoulders."

"Right," Chadwick answered grimly. "I have to admit, I'm glad I'm not handling this one by myself."

So that was the reason for the lessening of tension. Though the man sitting across from him seemed sincere, Luke wondered how long the geniality would last. He tapped his pencil point on the desk. "I'll get the librarian to start assembling our weekend reading."

The gray-haired Valkyrie who ran the firm's law library could get her teeth into this one. They'd have enough citations to keep them busy for weeks.

"Good. She likes you better than she likes me." Chadwick dropped his hands and seemed to relax. Then he gave a counterfeit groan. "Weekend reading? Hell, I just remembered."

Luke's gaze narrowed. Suddenly all the cockiness of the ladies' man was back, almost as though he'd dredged it up intentionally.

"I had a lot of other things planned for the weekend." Chadwick grinned. "Such as comforting our beautiful neighbor over dinner, with a fine brandy and maybe some soft music."

"You have a date with Alexandra?"

"Not yet. But I figured I could somehow manage one," Chadwick answered confidently.

Luke clenched his back teeth and felt the muscle in his jaw contract. He told himself the anger seething inside him was not envy, nor was it jealousy. "I'm sure you could. You're a master at seduction, aren't you?"

West studied him for a minute. "Yeah, I've been told I have talent. Why? Are you interested in Alexandra, yourself?"

"She's not my type," Luke answered shortly.

Luke had left work early and gone to the facility north of the city where he kept his small race car in storage. He was looking forward to having his house, with its own garages, finished.

Now, back at the condo, he maneuvered the tarp-shrouded trailer into two parking spaces at the edge of the complex. He got out of his car and locked it. Then he checked and tightened the ropes holding the canvas cover.

"Hi, Luke."

The kid was right behind him and he hadn't heard a thing. Once he would have been alert to the presence of a mosquito. It was disconcerting to discover that the sharp edge he'd had as a naval intelligence officer was definitely gone. Not that he needed it.

His life now was as placid as a stagnant pond. Occasionally he regretted the loss of exhilaration and excitement. A shrink would probably say he hung on to the idea of adventure in his life by racing.

"How are you, David?"

"Fine, I guess." He jammed his hands into the pockets of his jeans. "My mom says you're building a house."

He turned to smile at the boy as he gave a last jerk on the tarp. "Not me. I never could set a nail."

David blushed and retreated a step or two. "I— uh...I meant—"

Luke felt a guilty rush at the boy's embarrassment. He'd forgotten how hard it was to be a kid, and almost impossible to distinguish between adult teasing and seriousness.

He remembered similar incidents in his own childhood. The memories were painful, even now. He, too, had gone through his formative years without a father and he remembered how it felt to say or do some-

thing silly and awkward just because he didn't quite
know how to talk to a man.

He reached out to touch David's shoulder. "I know
what you meant, David. I'm sorry. I thought I was
kidding, but I'm clearly out of practice and not very
good at it."

The color retreated from David's cheeks. "That's
okay. Are you gonna have a dog when you move?"

"I've thought about getting a dog," Luke admitted. He paused and leaned back on his palms against
the trailer. He crossed his feet at the ankles and said
thoughtfully, "I've never had one, have you? What's
your favorite breed?"

"You've never had a dog?" David's voice rose in
disbelief on the last word.

"No, my mom worked. She said it wasn't fair to
leave a dog alone all day in an apartment."

"What about your dad?"

"My dad took off when I was a baby."

"Gee, I'm sorry," David said. Unconsciously he
mimicked Luke's posture, leaning against a fender. "I
had a golden retriever when I was little. She was actually my dad's dog. But she was old, and she died.
And then my dad—well, we moved here and you can't
have a pet in the condos."

One minute David's unhappiness was marked, but
then abruptly he straightened his slouch and shrugged
off any trace of self-pity. Luke saw the maturity
emerge that so astonished him in this kid.

"Goldens are good dogs," David went on knowl-
edgeably. "They make great watchdogs but they're not
vicious at all. And if you get a female, she won't roam

like a male would. She'll pretty much stay on your property."

Luke nodded, taking the boy's opinion very seriously. David was a bright kid. He'd probably studied the subject in detail. "I'll look into a golden," he said and meant it. "This house is going to fulfill a lot of dreams I had when I was a kid."

"So I guess you'll have a basketball goalpost, too?"

"I haven't thought about that. Tell you what. The house is not far from here. It overlooks the Hooch," he told the boy, nicknaming the Chattahoochee River that was the northern boundary of the city. "If your mom says it's all right, I'll take you over there tomorrow and you can see if there's a good spot for one."

David lit up at the suggestion. "Okay. That'd be great."

"You want to see something else that was a dream of mine?" Luke's question was rhetorical. While they talked, David's gaze had frequently flashed to the tarpaulin-covered trailer, but the boy was too well-mannered to appear overtly curious.

"Your race car?" he guessed.

Luke busied himself with the knots. "Yeah. She's been in storage in Marietta. I'll tow her to the garage tomorrow to give her a good going-over before the races."

The last knot on Luke's side came free. "Let me get the other side. Then grab that edge," Luke said, moving around the trailer. David stood ready until Luke said, "Okay." Together they flipped back the tarp.

David gasped in awe. The reflection of the sun on chrome could have hurt his eyes. "Gosh." He touched the shining hood reverently, ran his fingers down the fender. "Does it need polishing or anything?" he asked hopefully.

Luke pretended to ponder. "It probably could use a touch-up. I've got a chamois inside. Come on."

Alexandra was in her studio. It had taken her all morning to rearrange and reorganize her equipment and files, and most of the afternoon to clean up the mess. David had helped her for a while, but he had disappeared an hour or so earlier. She wondered where he'd gone.

She ran a flannel-covered brush briskly over the hardwood floor one last time, and sat back on her heels to admire her work. Charcoal had been crushed and ground into the grain. The wood now shone with a fresh coat of wax. Watercolors had been splattered onto windows and shelves. She had scrubbed and polished.

An hour later, she sat in front of her drawing board with a charcoal pencil in her hand. Waning sunlight poured through the window behind her.

But inspiration was as dry as last season's fruitcake. She sighed and tossed aside the pencil. She was feeling guilty for lying to Luke last night. He was a nice person and he had been kind to David; he didn't deserve her slight. She had no interest in dating him but she could have been more considerate.

"Mom, Luke's been showing me his car. Can I ask him to come to dinner?"

Her first inclination was to say no. But then, inviting him to dinner might alleviate some of her guilt. Mentally she reviewed her menu. "All right. If he understands that we're only having salads, tell him we'll be eating about six-thirty."

"Right."

"David." She called him back. "Knock on Mr. Chadwick's door and invite him, too."

His response was less than enthusiastic. "Aw, Mo-om."

"They were both very kind to us last night. And they work together. It would be rude to ask one without asking the other."

"Okay." David disappeared.

He was back in five minutes. "Mr. Chadwick isn't home, Mom," he told her with a bright smile. "And Luke says he likes salads."

Alexandra heard the doorbell. "I'll get it," David called.

A few seconds later, Luke came into the kitchen. "May I help?" he asked.

Alexandra glanced up from filling deviled eggs for a relish tray that held carrot and celery sticks, pickles and olives. She had made chicken salad and stuffed it into fresh tomatoes and piled potato salad on crisp Boston lettuce. Instead of hot bread, she had made cheese straws and was serving crackers.

Luke was still dressed in his suit and tie. Again she was reminded that he was larger than she'd thought. She had to take a breath before she could answer.

"Thanks, no. I have everything under control. I hope David made it clear that this is a casual meal."

Luke got the hint. He took off his jacket and hung it over the back of a chair. "That's the best kind." The kitchen was identical to his but she had added a small table for two. "Do you mind if I watch?"

"No, of course not," she said quickly.

He pulled the chair around to face her and loosened his tie. "It's been a long time since I sat in anybody's kitchen."

She gave him a restless smile. Her hair was pulled back in a loose ponytail. The ends curled as did the strands that had escaped to frame her face. She had on khaki slacks, a yellow oxford shirt with the sleeves rolled to her elbows and supple, well-worn penny loafers.

On her trim figure, the tailored clothing lost all vestige of the original masculine intent. Her hips had just enough curve; her breasts, just enough fullness; and between the two, her waist was nipped in sharply by a narrow brown belt.

Luke could see his presence was making her nervous and he wasn't sure why. But it was such an uncharacteristic reaction from this composed, self-possessed woman that he took a certain pleasure in it. He smiled to himself. Call it reprisal for those fleeting morning glimpses of another creature entirely.

But he wasn't getting off scot-free. He was too alert to the smooth and graceful movements of her hands, making him wonder precisely how clever those hands were. His gaze fixed on the clean, straight line of her spine, her long legs, her sweetly rounded bottom.

You lecherous fraud, he derided himself. *So she's not your type, huh?*

"Would you like a glass of wine?"

The beautiful honey-smooth voice intruded upon his fixation. "Hm-m-m?" he responded.

She had turned. The emerald eyes were looking at him, a puzzled expression in their depths. "I'm afraid wine is all I have." She raised her hand to look at a dab of the egg filling, clinging to her thumb. Her pink tongue darted out, and he felt the force of an electric shock.

Good God, she had an erotic way about her. And the odd thing was, she seemed totally unaware of her effect. He cleared his throat. "Wine sounds good. May I pour a glass for you?"

"Yes, please." She returned to her task.

While he found the glasses and poured the drinks, Alexandra finished the eggs, put them into the refrigerator and washed her hands. He handed her the glass and lifted his own in a silent toast. At the same time, he vowed to himself that he would not conjure up impossible fantasies about this woman.

Alexandra realized that sitting down or standing up, Luke took up too much space in her compact kitchen. "Let's go into the other room and enjoy our wine for a moment before I put the food out."

He followed her into the living room.

"Please, sit there on the sofa." She took a chair at right angles to him. The sun touched a corner of the glass-topped coffee table, reflecting into her eyes. She blinked against the glare and shifted her chair. "I enjoy daylight saving time, don't you?" she said.

He nodded, seeming to take her shallow comment seriously. He stretched his arm along the back of the sofa. "Yes. I like getting home from work before it gets dark outside."

She was unable to take her eyes off that long arm. His fingers were unusually long. Strong, capable, that was how his hand looked. Dark hair and a slim gold watch peeped out from beneath his cuff. She took a deep sip of wine to moisten her dry throat. "On the other hand, if the sun went down earlier, it might cool off enough for us to sit on the terrace. We don't get to use it much except in the spring or fall." Lord, she sounded like a ninny. Thank goodness he didn't bother to answer that one.

She groped for another topic. What on earth was wrong with her? She rarely felt awkward in any environment, much less her own home.

She wished that West had been available. She'd known him longer and she felt several degrees more comfortable with him.

What had happened to David? He'd disappeared as soon as Luke had arrived. She was definitely irked. This invitation was his idea in the first place. His leaving them alone like this was a bit obvious. She would have to speak to him.

At last, with some determination, she put on her best hostess face. "Tell me more about the races at Road Atlanta. David is so excited about your offering us tickets."

Luke smiled down into his wine, then took a swallow. When he raised his eyes to hers, she felt a sudden shock to her system. The horn-rimmed frames usually shadowed his expression, but from this angle the light from the window illuminated the piercing gray gaze completely.

His gaze held amusement, besides the intelligence, the cunning, the keen perception. She felt sorry for any witnesses being cross-examined by Luke Quinlan. When he began to speak, she had to force herself to focus on the words.

"For one thing, it won't be like watching the Indy 500 on Memorial Day. Vintage racers are primarily hobbyists and we treat our cars like babies. If they're damaged or destroyed, they can never be replaced. Most of us only take them out of storage a few times a year."

"I see." There was another gap in the conversation. His long legs were stretched out, crossed at the ankles, his feet only inches from hers. She had never seen him relaxed like this. The loosening of that controlled rigidity she associated with him added remarkably to his appeal. She looked away.

"How did you become interested in them?" Her voice sounded flimsy to her own ears.

"When I was a kid, a friend of my mother's owned a garage. He taught me to tinker. Then when I was in the navy, I had a friend who raced."

"You're from West Virginia, aren't you? What part?"

Before Luke could do more than nod, the doorbell rang again. Thankful for the distraction, Alexandra excused herself. She reached the door at the same time David decided to put in an appearance. He opened it.

West Chadwick stood there, a bottle of wine in his hand. "Hi, Alexandra, David. I stopped by to see if you've recovered from yesterday's ordeal."

His gaze went past her and his eyes narrowed. She knew what he saw. Luke was plainly visible from the front door, lounging on the sofa as though he'd been planted there. West's handsome face was noncommittal.

"Come in, West," Alexandra said. "David looked for you earlier to invite you to supper. If you don't have plans, you're welcome to join us."

"You're sure it won't be any trouble?" He was already moving past her. David followed.

"Not a bit of trouble." She was left holding the door and watching their backs.

The invitation had been a major mistake, she acknowledged an hour later as she went to the kitchen to make a pot of coffee.

The two men had circled each other like wary tigers all evening. She was astonished at the extent of the discord between them.

They worked together every day, and since West had been the one to tell Luke about the availability of the condo, she had assumed they were friends. It soon became obvious that her assumption was totally wrong.

The opening maneuver in their conversational competition had been ambiguous, apparently concerning some work they were doing for a fractious client. They had seemed mostly in accord on that one.

But then weekend reading had been mentioned in relation to the client.

"I didn't think I would see you until Monday. Didn't you say you had a lot of research to do?" West inquired in a biting tone.

"I said *we* have research to do. The reading material will be ready tomorrow morning," Luke responded easily. "I'm picking it up at the office. I'm sorry, but I am afraid it's going to put a dent in your social agenda for the rest of the weekend."

The evening went downhill from there. Alexandra had no idea what they were talking about, but she had an idea some of their taunting comments centered on her. She grew irritated with the sniping remarks they made to each other, as well.

David quickly became Luke's champion—as though Luke needed one—agreeing with everything he said even when he didn't understand.

As a result, Alexandra felt that she had to be conciliatory toward West. And West loved that—he kept looking over at Luke with a smug, canarylike smile. Luke responded with a frown as black as night.

Toward her, they were both overly solicitous. She liked that even less. West held her chair when she sat down at the table.

"May I pour you some wine, Alexandra?" Luke asked as soon as her glass was empty.

"I'll be glad to help with the dishes," offered West when they'd finished eating.

She wanted to scream. *This is ridiculous. You two are not dogs and I am not a bone.*

A mistake, she repeated to herself as she gave the key in the new dead-bolt lock a vicious twist. The invitation had been a big blunder, one she would never make again. She dropped her keys into her purse and headed for her bedroom. She needed an early night.

After the robbery last night, the cleaning job she'd had to do today and the frustrating conversation with the insurance company, she had to top it off by playing hostess to Siskel and Ebert.

The telephone rang. She put a knee on the bed and leaned across to snatch up the receiver. "Hello?" she answered.

She was met with nothing but dead air. She slammed down the receiver, muttered a curse aimed at rude people who got a wrong number and hung up without apologizing. She started to strip off her clothes and the phone rang again. "Hello...? Hello!"

There was no answer, but this time the air was not dead. A living, breathing presence was on the line. It whispered corruption, which sinuously wound through the twists and turns of technological connections to reach her ears.

Alexandra slammed down the receiver again. She hoped she never had to listen to such malice again.

Luke decided it was the most uncomfortable evening he'd spent in years. He hadn't deliberately set out to wangle a dinner invitation, but he'd had no reservations about accepting when one was offered.

Then Chadwick had walked through the door, believing that Luke was intentionally trying to cut him out and reacting like an arrogant buck whose favorite doe had just gone to the water hole with a deer from another herd.

Luke usually replied to verbal jabs with restraint; his control in tense situations was one of his strengths as a lawyer. But he had grown so accustomed to their rivalry at the office that he responded accordingly.

And when Chadwick had started his not-very-subtle pursuit of Alexandra, Luke had suddenly been reminded of the other lawyer's rather careless reputation with women. He'd reacted with uncharacteristic heat at the thought of Alexandra's becoming Chadwick's next victim.

As the evening had worn on, he could feel her tension building. Her dismay, and her frequent glances toward David, had brought out Luke's protective instincts, making him more aggravated with Chadwick than he ever was at the office.

He wasn't proud of the way he had acted. His usual solution to clashes like this was to pull back, to try to get an objective handle on things. For some reason, however, last night he couldn't seem to establish one iota of objectivity.

But when he had realized that sides were being chosen, and David was ending up on his side, against his mother, he was appalled. He got out of there as quickly as he could.

Chadwick left, too, both of them having finally gotten the message that they weren't pleasant company. Alexandra hadn't bothered to hide her relief as she showed them the door. She probably didn't want to see either of them for a long time.

Luke told himself that suited him fine. He wouldn't be the cause of conflict between mother and son. And she really *wasn't* his type.

* * *

Luke had made arrangements to meet his builder at the house site the next morning. He wanted a quick walk-through before he went to the office. As he headed for his car, he saw the teenager riding his bicycle in the parking area in front of the condos.

He swallowed a groan when he remembered his invitation to the boy, but he reconciled himself to fulfilling the promise. After today, however, he told himself, that would be the end of it. He would steer clear of the boy and his mother.

"Morning, David. Did you ask for permission to go to the house with me?"

"Yes, sir," answered the boy. He took a half turn around the lot and ended up beside Luke's car. He brought the bike to a halt and rested his forearms across the handlebars. "Mom didn't think it was such a good idea. She said I might get in your way."

Luke looked at David's downcast features for a minute. He should have asked her himself, rather than leave it to the boy. Hell, he owed her an apology, anyway. "Wait here. I'll see if I can change her mind."

The ringing bell sounded hollow through the thickness of the door. He looked back at the teenager who stood beside his bike, watching hopefully but trying not to show he was watching.

At last she answered. She was dressed for town in a tailored linen dress and flats. Her hair was slicked away from her face—no appealing tendrils this morning. She was not smiling.

"Good morning, Alexandra," he said quietly.

"Good morning."

"I hope you'll change your mind and let David go with me to the house." She hesitated and he added, "He won't be in my way, and I have to be at the office later. I'll have him back in about an hour."

"I don't suppose he told you that we have plans to shop for school clothes today."

Luke's mouth twitched. "No, he didn't mention shopping. He said you thought he'd be in my way. I wouldn't have asked him to go if that were the case," he told her.

"Did you ask or did he invite himself?"

Luke leaned his elbow against the doorjamb and worried his jaw with his knuckles, but he couldn't keep the smile off his face. "Well, technically, I asked."

Alexandra looked past Luke's shoulder to the parking area and sighed. "I suppose he'll complain all morning if I drag him to the mall." A good mother would probably use this opportunity to reinforce a sense of responsibility. But this morning she was too exhausted to enforce anything. She had not slept well last night. "All right," she said, giving in. She started to turn away.

"I have an idea," he said. Almost reluctantly, she thought.

She crossed her arms and leaned against the other side of the door. "I'm afraid to ask," she said with a wry expression.

"Why don't you follow us in your car? I'd like you to see the house, too. Then you can take David shopping and I can head downtown directly from there."

Alexandra realized with some amazement that she wanted to go. "Do you work every Saturday?" she asked in order to gain a bit of thinking time.

"Just about." He smiled ruefully. "So, how about it?"

She hesitated for only a moment more, then she said, "Let me get my purse and keys."

Alexandra had left Luke talking to the builder while she explored. The house was almost complete, and she was impressed.

She was standing at the edge of a wide redwood deck, cantilevered over a slope leading down to the river. The wood was raw right now, but she could picture the weathered gray patina it would have in a year or so. A hot tub had been installed on one end of the deck, shielded by a latticed screen of the same wood.

Behind her, the soaring walls of glass and rock and cedar were spectacular. The house was shaped like open arms, just large enough to be impressive, but not so large that it lost any warmth. Minutes from the interstate highway, the quiet, bucolic setting, among pine and oak and dogwood trees, was remarkable. Every room overlooked water, or would when the pool on the other side of the house was filled.

"How do you like it?"

She hadn't heard him approach, but he was standing right beside her. She smiled. "It's a wonderful house. Did you have an architect?"

"Yes, but I'm afraid I was pretty adamant about what I wanted. I've been dreaming of this for a long time." He looked around with obvious satisfaction. "I was lucky to find someone who could translate my dream and a good builder to make it real."

"When will it be finished?"

"A month to six weeks, they tell me."

She looked around, realizing suddenly that the man Luke had come to meet was gone. "Are you through here?" she asked.

"Yes." When she would have moved to leave, he stopped her with a word. "Wait."

He was clearly uncomfortable and she was afraid she knew what was coming. She was right.

"Alexandra, I hope you'll accept my apology for last night," he said formally.

Her shapely chin came up at the disagreeable memory his apology evoked. "It was—a peculiar evening. I thought you and West were friends or I never would have invited you together." And won't again, she added silently as she tightened her lips.

Luke saw the strain around Alexandra's pretty mouth and wished he could read her mind. He propped one hip on the heavy railing, so he could look directly at her elegant profile. Though she was tall, only a few inches short of his six feet, her bone structure was delicate and feminine. The breeze off the river tugged at a strand of her hair, trying valiantly to loosen it from its tight coil.

"I'm not sure how to explain our association. West and I started with the firm on the same day. We work together amiably on some things but I'm afraid we're deadly rivals on others." She glanced at him and he smiled to diminish the sting of his statement. "You just happened to catch us on a bad day."

"Funny, I got the impression that your disagreement had something to do with me." Her eyebrows lifted in query, then she returned her attention to the swiftly flowing water below.

"Your instincts are good," he answered, choosing his words carefully. "We had been talking earlier about the effect the break-in had on you. I guess we were both feeling protective."

She turned to face him, her lovely green eyes sincere and beguiling. "I didn't like having my child caught in the middle of your disagreement."

The breeze finally had its way; the strand of hair came loose and whipped across her mouth. She brushed at it.

"I didn't like that, either. Again, I apologize."

"David doesn't particularly care for West, and he seems to think you're a cross between Geronimo and Gandhi. Nevertheless, I won't have him behaving rudely."

"I understand." He finally succumbed to temptation. He separated the strand from her moist lips and tucked it behind her ear.

The contact of his fingers with her cheek froze them both into place. For an eternal interval, neither of them spoke; neither of them breathed.

"Mom! Luke! Where are you?"

The spell was broken. Maybe it never happened. "Here," called Alexandra. "On the deck."

"Isn't this a terrific house?" David enthused. "Luke, I found a perfect place for your basketball goal. Come on. I'll show you."

"Great," Luke said.

"Then we have to go," added Alexandra.

The two adults walked quickly after David, through the house to the driveway, where both cars were parked. The site for the goalpost was pointed out and approved.

With a feeling that she had just escaped a nameless danger, Alexandra climbed into her station wagon and fastened her seat belt. She and David left for the mall.

Luke got away as quickly as possible, too.

Chapter 4

Alexandra alternated between pacing her living room and looking out the window in the kitchen while she waited for Luke to come home. She had to talk to him.

Starting high school, which should have been a milestone for David, had passed almost automatically two days ago. She had thought her son might be apprehensive about entering a new school, or enthusiastic, or nervous. She'd been prepared to deal with any one of those emotions. What she hadn't expected was indifference.

He saw the first day of school as something to get through before he could continue with his two main interests—his matchmaking efforts on her behalf, which he assumed were subtle but in reality were nothing of the kind, and his avid interest in anything Luke Quinlan did or said. Of course, the two were essentially intertwined, since her son had decided that Luke was the logical target of the matchmaking.

Even when the new television, VCR and stereo had been delivered, he'd spared barely any attention for the latest in new technology.

She had tried talking to David first, hoping she could avoid this discussion with Luke. But neither serious discussion nor a direct maternal order discouraged David's cheerful efforts to get her and Luke together.

Curiously, she trusted Luke where David was concerned. Trusted him to do the right thing. He might be unaware of David's growing determination but he had taken a sincere interest in the boy.

Alexandra, however, didn't want David to bank on anyone other than himself. Or her.

Besides, Luke had made inroads in her own life that made her uncomfortable.

A week had passed since the trip to his house. A week that had found David living in the man's pocket every available minute; and, when he wasn't with Luke, he was arranging encounters.

"Luke's on his way to get a pizza, Mom, and he's asked us to go along."

"I told Luke you made the best homemade ice cream in the world, Mom. I invited him to help turn the crank."

During that week, Luke had also introduced her son to the world of mechanical things, powerful cars and racing engines. Men things. One evening, he had taken David to the garage where his vintage car was being serviced.

David had come home that night, impatient to explain to his mother the importance of testing every part of the awesome silver car, since it had been in storage for the better part of the year.

He had returned covered with grease and a grin and more excited than she'd seen him in four years. For that she had to be grateful, didn't she?

He had regaled her nonstop with a description of the cars they'd seen, the things they'd done, how smart Luke was, how many friends he had.

He had extolled Luke Quinlan's virtues until she was nearly sick of the man's name.

Nearly, but not nearly enough.

For those seven days, too, had left Alexandra unable to forget the passing touch of a man's fingers on her cheek. The warm ribbons of heat that had wound their way through her bloodstream were unmistakably the result of his light caress. She'd thought herself, her emotions, her life, secure.

And suddenly she was not.

She had won her autonomy after a struggle of monumental proportions. She'd fought not simply for independence from financial worry, although that was significant, but to free herself from the dependence upon another person for happiness.

The void left in her life by Daniel's death had been wide and deep, and all passion had been exhausted on the long journey back from that black pit. She would not allow anyone to tempt her.

Luke would soon be moving to his house on the river. Then they might never see him again.

She halted in her tracks. Where had that concept come from? *David,* she amended. *David* might never see Luke again. There was no "we" about it.

She had decided to be honest with Luke. She wanted him to be aware of David's vulnerability. She wanted him to start pulling away gradually.

When she saw his car pull into his space, she headed for the front door. She paused to smooth her hair, then reached for the knob. "Luke, I wonder if I could talk—" She broke off.

He looked like hell. His hair was standing on end; his eyes were bloodshot. The man she'd once thought of as rigid was slouched over an armload of books. "Yes, Alexandra?" he asked impatiently.

"Uh, nothing. I see you've brought work home. What I wanted to discuss can wait." She started to go back inside, but during their exchange, West Chadwick's sporty car had driven in. He got out and joined them.

He looked as bad as Luke but he managed a smile and greeting for her. "How are you, Alexandra?"

She felt almost relieved at his presence. At least she could depend on West to be friendly. She smiled warmly. "Better than the two of you are, I imagine. You both look exhausted."

"Yeah. We—" he nodded at Luke, who had paused at his door and was fishing in his pocket for his key "—have some contract work for a big-shot client that has to be done yesterday. You look great. Got a date?"

She had dressed in nubby silk slacks and an ecru blouse. She'd told herself she wanted to present a dignified front when she talked to Luke. In fact, the outfit was one of her most becoming. "Thank you. No, not a date."

"You coming over here to work, or are you going to stand there and socialize?" Luke asked West with cold, active dislike in his voice.

Actually, most of the dislike was for himself. He needed to have his butt kicked from here to the Hooch. Alexandra had said she wanted to talk. Had she dressed like that for him? Why hadn't *he* paid her a compliment? Why hadn't he been cordial, at least, instead of sounding like a surly bastard?

Because his mind was on other things. He was furious over being assigned to this client. The man was more trouble than anyone Luke had ever worked with.

Before he and West had been ordered to work with this man, Luke had been drawing up a set of contracts for a young entrepreneur. But to Bolton, the senior partner, the young man's business wasn't as important as the big shot's. When Luke had tried to protest, the senior partner had glared at him and told him to turn the young man's file over to a junior.

He'd backed off. Then he'd cursed himself for a coward. Someday...

"I'll be there," West said, interrupting Luke's thoughts. "In a few minutes."

Luke heard a coldness and outrage to match his own.

Alexandra left her studio at midnight, flipping off the lights with one hand while massaging her neck with the other. She had been working on a series of kids' greeting cards for a children's hospital. And they were completed. She could deliver them to the printer the next morning after she dropped David off at school.

Now she needed a little self-indulgence. Cookies and milk and a long soak in a hot tub sounded about right. She started the bathwater, squirted in a generous amount of jasmine-scented gel and headed for the kitchen.

She had just poured her milk and bitten into a vanilla wafer, when the doorbell rang. She looked at the clock. Who on earth would be ringing her bell at this hour?

She checked the peephole, then unlocked the door. "Do you know what time it is?" she challenged with one hand on her hip.

Luke stood with his forearm propped on the jamb, his free hand in his pocket. The white dress shirt was wrinkled but the cuffs were still fastened. His tie had been loosened but not removed.

In contrast, she knew she looked like a castaway. She'd exchanged her slacks and blouse for cutoffs and a T-shirt.

"I saw the light come on in your kitchen," Luke explained. His voice sounded unfamiliar even to his own ears. Except for the brief glimpses of her in the mornings, he'd never seen Alexandra Prescott less than perfectly groomed.

Tonight her lipstick had been eaten off, her hair was tangled and she wore no shoes. He realized that even in rags she would be just what she was, an incredibly beautiful woman.

He smiled to himself. The disreputable shorts and stretched T-shirt spoke to him in more ways than the obvious one—that she was one hell of a sexy woman. They said that here, also, was a woman with unique allure.

He was surprised and delighted to see that she didn't have to be impeccable every minute.

There was a crumb of something on her lower lip. As he watched, she licked it away.

He realized that he was staring. And she was waiting for him to continue. "I wondered—that is—what did you want to discuss with me?"

She looked at him for a minute. He knew what she saw. Beard stubble and bleary eyes. She must have taken pity on him for she smiled and opened the door wider. "Would you like some cookies and milk?"

"Cookies and milk?" he said.

She stepped back. "You know, the traditional bedtime snack. Come inside. You're letting the air-conditioning out."

Moving in slow motion, he obeyed.

"Go into the kitchen. I left water running. I'll be right back."

She disappeared in the direction of the bedrooms. He did as he was told. In the kitchen he saw the glass of milk and a box of vanilla wafers on the table. "You weren't kidding," he said when she returned. She had taken time, he noticed, to brush her hair and secure it at the nape of her neck with a barrette.

"I never kid about cookies and milk," she said almost playfully. She took another glass from the cabinet and poured milk into it. Then she sat at the table and reached into the box for another cookie. "Are you going to eat standing up or did you want to take it with you?"

He slumped into the chair across from her. "Sorry. I'm in a stupor, I guess. And before I forget my name, here." He reached into his shirt pocket and, with two fingers, pulled out a pair of tickets. He tossed them onto the table between them.

Alexandra saw the Road Atlanta logo and her spirits fell. So much for pulling back gradually from David. "I'd almost forgotten," she said guardedly. "Labor Day is this coming weekend."

"Right." He delved in the box and took out several cookies, popped one into his mouth whole and chewed. Then he lifted the tall glass of milk and drank in thirsty gulps. "That's good. I forget the last time I had a bedtime snack. What did you want to talk to me about?"

She slid her glass around in its condensation. Then she must have realized what she was doing. She went to a cabinet and came back with two paper napkins.

"David," she finally said when she had reseated herself. "First, let me tell you that I'm grateful for the time you've spent with him. Learning about the cars firsthand has been a wonderful experience."

"I've enjoyed his showing interest in my car. Most kids his age are more into MTV." He remembered a woman he'd dated last year. She was divorced with two kids who spent so much time in front of the television, their complexions were pasty. He thought Alexandra did a good job balancing her son's activities.

"I appreciate that." Suddenly Alexandra stood up and moved around the kitchen with restless steps.

"How do I say this without sounding like a jerk?" she said almost to herself.

"Come on, spit it out." He smiled. "I can take it."

"Okay." She took a deep breath. "To you this is a temporary friendship initially pushed onto you by an overeager teenager. You've been patient and kind. But what happens to him when you move? Luke, David is becoming too dependent on you."

He took off his glasses and rubbed his eyes before answering. "You don't think you're exaggerating?" He slipped the glasses back on.

"I'm afraid not. Fourteen is such a vulnerable age. You'll soon be moving away. I realize that you wouldn't deliberately..." She let her voice fade off. "You'll get caught up in your own life. It worries me that he might be hurt."

He took another bite of vanilla wafer and chewed. "Are you sure that's all that bothers you about David's behavior?"

She paused, looking at him, trying to read his expression. But she couldn't. As usual, he had control of his features. "I don't know what you mean."

"I'm talking about his attempts to throw us together."

She hadn't intended to discuss that subject. "Don't be ridiculous. He's a child."

"For a child, he does a pretty good job of dropping hints. You told me that you don't date, but maybe you should. Maybe if you went out occasionally, he wouldn't be so fixated about finding you a man."

"I don't *want* a man," she snapped. How had he managed to turn this around and make her the villain? "I've had a husband. He died. Now I have a son and a fulfilling career."

"And that's enough for you?"

She raised her chin. "More than enough," she said decisively.

"I thought we'd be there by now," David said. "How come they call it Road Atlanta when it's so far away?" He'd been squirming for the past thirty miles.

Alexandra raised her sunglasses and gave him a short, but telling, look. "Sorry," he said. "I guess I asked that before, didn't I?"

"At least a dozen times," she affirmed. She was not feeling terribly charitable toward her son; his attempts at matchmaking were becoming an irritant. She had bargained with him—stop trying to throw Luke and her together, in exchange for this weekend at the races. He'd promised, but she wasn't holding her breath.

David flopped back against the seat. She'd convinced him to wear shorts because of the weather and his berry-brown legs twitched with impatience.

As usual, Labor Day weekend in Georgia was classic southern summer. The sky was a beautiful, clear blue bowl, and the weather was hot—sweltering, scorching, sizzling hot.

From the radio, the announcer informed them that the stalled high over South Carolina meant the heat wave would continue, with no relief in sight. The sun beat down on the car, taxing the air-conditioning to its limit.

This was not the kind of day to spend outside, even for a national celebration. She had dressed as coolly as possible without wearing her bathing suit, in scarlet Bermuda shorts and an oversize white camp shirt knotted at the waist but barely touching her anyplace else. Her sneakers were a patriotic navy blue.

The traffic began to slow as they approached the track. She followed the directions Luke had given her and finally found a place to park.

David scanned the area, getting his bearings quickly. "The grid is this way," he told her. According to David, the grid was the name given to the area where cars and racers prepared for the races. They approached a rise overlooking the activity. The smell of high-octane exhaust was stronger here and the noise of revving engines was bone-vibrating.

"Gosh, Mom, *look* at that! Isn't it *great?*"

She grinned at him. It was a sight to behold. These cars weren't the analogous formula racers seen on television from Indianapolis.

Dashing, splashy, jaunty, they belonged to another age, an age of individualism. Many of them were very old indeed, though the shining paint and flawless maintenance made the cars look as if they had been assembled yesterday.

Alexandra was glad she'd taken the time last night to look through the books David had borrowed from Luke. Neither the written explanation, nor the color photographs, could have prepared her for the circus-like atmosphere, but at least she wasn't at a total loss.

She recognized several of the models from the illustrations—a Porsche, a Jaguar. The sleek lines and older, more debonair designs were particularly beautiful to her artist's eye.

The orbiting support groups—mechanics, sponsors, groupies, moral supporters—seemed as diverse as the cars themselves. Huge custom-built tractor-trailers vied with rusty pickup trucks. People swarmed everywhere, like a hive of energetic bees—around the cars, under the hoods, on rolling dollies beneath the bodies. Some sat in lawn chairs watching the parade—colorful tents or large sun umbrellas provided shade—some picnicked, others strolled around greeting old friends, meeting new ones.

Alexandra's fingers itched for her sketch pad. She touched the tote bag slung over her shoulder to reassure herself that she hadn't forgotten to bring it.

"Hi," said a voice behind her. "Did you have any trouble finding a place to park?"

"Hey, Luke, you got new glasses," David said. "I like 'em."

Alexandra turned, a smile ready.

Her smile collapsed. Indeed, she was hard-pressed not to gape at the devastatingly good-looking man at her side. The night of the robbery, she had thought he'd looked unlike himself with his jacket off and his tie loosened. When he'd come for dinner, he had seemed more relaxed, less rigid. Late the other night, sitting at her kitchen table, she'd seen yet another side to him. She'd seen him several times lately in casual situations.

But she'd never seen him like this. Surely a new pair of glasses wouldn't make so much difference.

She fought to control her features, hoping neither of them noticed her shock.

He shook David's hand—a nice man-to-man thing to do—and said something to the boy. But she was deaf to their conversation.

There was nothing rigid about his easy smile, which activated a slash in his cheek. His hair was ruffled by the wind. And he never looked like this in his Brooks Brothers suits.

The white T-shirt had been washed a few times. In hot water. It molded to his broad shoulders, chest and upper arms like a lover's touch. The jeans must have been washed in the same load; the way they fit his trim hips and strong thighs left little of his sexual definition to the imagination.

As David had noted, the conservative horn-rimmed glasses had been exchanged for a tinted pair with aviator-style rims. The wing-tip shoes had been replaced by well-worn running shoes. He slid his hands into the back pockets of his jeans and stood, hipshot, his body easy and oddly graceful, devoid of the stiffness and severity she had associated with him.

The man was the epitome of masculinity. Lusty, tempting, virile masculinity.

The smells, the noise, the activity faded into a white shadowy backdrop. For the first time in four long years, she experienced earnest stirrings of hunger, of sexual awareness. Not just ribbons of heat, prompted by a brief caress on the cheek, but true desire. Familiar and yet alien, foreign; an emotion sensed, not felt.

Her palms were damp, her breathing, shallow. Her breasts seemed full, her nipples, sensitive against the restriction of her bra.

Then he turned to her.

For a long moment, their gazes met. He read her awareness as easily as if it had been written on her forehead in capital letters.

And he grinned. Knowingly.

Alexandra was mortified.

"Is it okay, Mom?" David asked, wrenching her back to the present, back to the smelly, noisy racetrack, the hot sun, the dust.

She had no idea what her son was talking about. "What?" she said stupidly.

"Mo-om—"

"I've arranged for David to take a touring run around the track if it's all right with you."

"I guess it's all right," she said, still slightly at sea.

"Aw-right! Let's go, Luke."

Luke hesitated. "David, you see that woman down there by the car, the one in red overalls?" He pointed. When David nodded, he went on, "Her name is Maggie."

David looked at him. "Maggie?"

"Well, her name is Margaret but if you call her that, she'll black your eye. Go down there and introduce yourself. Tell her your mom said yes. Here are your credentials." He pinned a plastic badge on David's shirt, a match to the one he wore. "Maggie will find you a helmet and I'll meet you there in a minute."

David ran down the shallow grade toward the grid, leaving them alone.

"I'll take care of him. It's quite safe, you know. This is only a drive-around. But even in a race, and as I told you, the people who own vintage cars are hobbyists first, racers second."

His tone was calm and unflappable, meant to be soothing to a nervous parent. But it had the opposite effect on her. His low, steady voice merely upped the temperature of her blood as it raced through her veins.

This was ridiculous. She had to get hold of herself. She wasn't an emotional adolescent, reacting to the captain of the football team. She forced a casual smile. "I'm not afraid. I appreciate your thinking of the treat. He'll love it. Where shall I meet you?"

"We'll come back to the grid. Maggie has fixed a picnic lunch for us. Or we can eat in the clubhouse tower if you'd prefer."

Alexandra looked down toward the grid, where her son stood talking to a tiny blonde in bright red coveralls. "Maggie is—"

He grinned, reactivating the slash. "My crew chief."

"A mechanic?"

"One of the best. Her father owned the garage in my hometown where I learned to tinker. She's always worked around the cars. Come on, I'll introduce you."

But Alexandra wasn't ready to descend into the hive of activity just yet. She needed to get back her equilibrium. "You go on. I'll wander around up here for a while."

Luke eyed her closely but she refused to let any emotion show on her face. "Are you all right?" he asked finally.

She gave a short dismissive laugh. "Of course. I'll meet you in—what?—fifteen minutes? Thirty?"

He glanced at his watch. "Make it thirty." From his pocket he took another plastic badge. "Here are your credentials. They'll get you into the grid area and the tower." He pointed to a tall building on a rise above them. "If you want a good view of this side of the track and the finish line, that's the place to be." He grinned and her breath stopped at the sight of his strong white teeth, his sensual mouth. "You can watch us go by. They have refreshments up there, too."

"Okay. Thanks. I'll see you later." She headed back toward the crowds with not a little bit of relief and pinned the badge to her collar.

Luke watched her go. She was different today, more relaxed. He smiled.

The breeze that wove its way through the pines was welcome on Alexandra's overheated face. She wandered to a concession stand and bought a soda. The cool drink quelled some of the turmoil in her belly. She was still shocked by her stormy reaction to him. More than shocked—she was stunned. It was so unlike her.

Why? She was often exposed to good-looking men, without making a fool of herself. She didn't gawk like a groupie at a rock concert. Perhaps it was the unexpected contrast between his office-lawyer persona and the racing enthusiast. Yes, surely that was the explanation.

She'd become accustomed to her straitlaced, quiet-spoken and stiff-backed neighbor. To suddenly be presented with a Kevin Costner clone...it was more than her logic could handle. Like accidentally coming upon the president of the United States in running shorts. That had been a shock, too.

She quit trying to rationalize her reaction, vowing to guard against its happening again.

On the other hand, she was both surprised and gladdened to realize that her sensuality hadn't been buried forever. At times recently, she'd begun to wonder if she would ever be attracted to a man again. She'd wondered when she went out with West and felt nothing except a slight warming, easily attributed to friendship.

West was also a handsome man. Maybe better-looking than Luke. With his dark coffee-colored hair and blue eyes, his easy grin and ambling, self-confident gait, he would even be called sexy by most women.

Foolish thoughts! Sexy was definitely not on her agenda. She quickened her step and set off toward the viewing tower. The large room at the top was filled with people. She edged toward the glass to look out over the track. Six cars sped by as she watched, obviously not racing one another, but going awfully fast, anyway. Either Luke and David had already passed or she was looking for the wrong car.

Then she spied the gleaming silver hood coming around a copse of pine trees. Sunlight on the windshield concealed their faces until they were almost beneath her. As the car slowed, preparing to turn back into the grid, she waved. But they didn't see her and her hand fell senselessly to her side.

There had been a look of unmitigated joy on the face of her son. It was an expression she hadn't seen in years. She watched the car until it stopped. Though she could no longer see details of their enjoyment, she saw the two exchange high fives.

Tears blurred the sight and she blinked them away, feeling unsettled and slightly guilty. Clearly the child was reveling in the company of a man.

Not very big for his age, David had not shown much interest in sports, except as a spectator. He hadn't had the benefit of the sort of masculine influence a coach would have provided to a fatherless boy. She was sorry David didn't like West Chadwick.

West was good company, fun to be with, she thought irrelevantly. And he seemed to be attracted to her. Or as attracted as a man like West could be. He hadn't a serious bone in his body. As far as she was concerned, that was his greatest appeal.

She could control her response around him. Whereas her emotions seemed to have a life of their own when Luke was nearby.

West was definitely the safest direction.

Alexandra retraced her steps. Suddenly, she shivered. All around her, people were laughing, shouting to be heard over the din. And she felt as alone as she'd ever felt. She quickened her steps. When she reached the crest of the hill overlooking the grid, a security man eyed her badge, then nodded and turned away.

David ran to meet her. "Hi, Mom. Did you see me?"

She hugged her son, grateful for his warmth. "I certainly did. I had a great view from the tower. Did you enjoy the trip?"

"It was rad, Mom. Totally awesome!"

She didn't have to be told that, thought Alexandra. Her son's face still glowed with animation. "So, have you decided to be a race car driver?" She successfully hid a delicate shudder.

He grinned. "Maybe someday."

Maggie was a surprise. What Alexandra had seen as blond was, in fact, prematurely white hair. In her early forties, she was a lovely woman. Where she swiped at perspiration on her face, the dust and grease were beginning to disguise her fine, delicate features. And she was very nice.

When Luke took David off to show him another car, Alexandra found herself alone with the woman.

Maggie opened the back of a van. She took out a folding table and began to set it up. Alexandra joined her. "What can I do?"

"The tablecloth and napkins are in the yellow basket."

Alexandra shook out the cloth and spread it on the table. "Luke tells me you are following in your father's footsteps." She indicated the toolbox on the ground with a wave of her hand.

Maggie gave her a brief, blank look, then understanding dawned. She chuckled. "Working on cars is a hobby. I'm a bank teller."

Alexandra was confused. "I'm sorry. I must have misunderstood."

"Luke probably said that my father taught me about cars. He taught Luke, too. We both grew up in the same little town in West Virginia." Maggie continued to talk as she handed Alexandra a handful of plastic tableware and reached into the van for the first of what seemed to be a dozen containers. "After I got married, I think Dad hoped Luke would take over his business but he went off to college, instead."

"And you both ended up in Atlanta."

Maggie nodded. "My husband was born here. He's a teacher at Piedmont High."

Alexandra, who had taken a large bowl of potato salad from Maggie, swung to face her. Here might be just the man to wean David from his dependency on Luke. "That's where David is going this year," she said delightedly. "He's a freshman."

"It's a good school. Morris teaches algebra and geometry and helps coach the soccer team."

David was impressed when he learned that Maggie's husband was a teacher, less so at the news that he was also a coach. During lunch, he peppered Maggie with questions, which she answered good-naturedly. But they were questions about cars, not school.

At one point, Alexandra tried to slow her son down, introduce the subject of Maggie's husband, the teacher. But it didn't work. And Maggie indicated that she didn't mind his curiosity.

Luke treated Maggie like a treasured friend—or an older sister. Alexandra didn't know why that pleased her, but it did. Their friends stopped by in a constant stream, friends they had known for years, friends they'd met this morning. Some were Maggie's friends;

some were Luke's. But Alexandra found out why Maggie had prepared so much food. Almost everyone who came picked up a sandwich, a brownie, a chicken leg, to munch on while they talked.

After they finished lunch, Alexandra helped Maggie pack up the van, then both women found a spot in the shade while Luke and David took a last walk to the Concours d'Elegance, the exhibition of display cars.

Alexandra took out her sketch pad.

"This is the first time I've ever known Luke to invite a woman to the track," said Maggie idly as she looked over Alexandra's shoulder.

Alexandra laughed. "He didn't invite me, he asked David. I'm just along as chauffeur." She hesitated. "This has been a wonderful experience for him. He doesn't often get to spend much time with men. He isn't particularly interested in sports, as you could probably tell."

"How did he—no, no—" She broke off and shook her head. "It's none of my business." She leaned over to see what Alexandra was doing. "Hey, that's good!"

Alexandra laughed. "Thank you. Sit over there on the edge of the trailer."

"You're going to draw me?"

"If you don't object."

"No, I guess not." But she didn't sound quite sure.

As she had done many times to make her subject feel comfortable, Alexandra began to talk easily. "You were asking about my husband? He was killed just over four years ago."

"Killed?"

"In a private plane crash."

"Poor kid. I know David's fourteen, but you don't look close to thirty yet."

"Thank you very, *very* much." Alexandra laughed. "I'm thirty-five."

"That's still pretty young." Maggie folded her hands in her lap and looked closely at Alexandra. "It must have been awfully hard for you," she said quietly.

"Yes," she responded. "I was young when we married. Daniel was a good provider. I went to art school until David was born. After his birth, all I had to do was keep the house, take care of the baby and spend the money Daniel provided." She couldn't help it—bitterness crept into her voice. The hand holding the pencil paused over the paper.

"There are women who would envy you."

"Then they've never had to cruise unprepared into the world of mortgages and taxes and business and insurance. After Daniel's death, I didn't have a clue how to get hospitalization, or what kind of house payments I could afford. I've had to learn everything myself." She took a deep breath and let it out. Then she smiled, briefly. "But I caught on, and luckily so did my drawings."

She touched the end of the pencil to her lip and stared off into the middle distance. "If I don't teach my child any other lesson, I intend to teach him to be independent. And not just financially. I relied too much on Daniel personally, as well. I don't intend to ever depend so much on anyone again."

Maggie's forehead tangled in a worried frown. "But we all need other people occasionally."

"Not me, not like that, not ever again. I don't blame Daniel—or maybe I do a little. But he certainly didn't plan on dying. I blame myself more for letting an untenable condition materialize solely because of my own ignorance."

There was a long silence. Alexandra got the strong impression that Maggie didn't approve of her philosophy.

The suspicion was confirmed when Maggie said, "I can understand your frustration, though I've been fortunate never to have gone through such an ordeal. Morris insists that I know as much as he about our personal business. But do you think the other part, the isolation, is good for you?"

Alexandra deliberated. "Perhaps not," she said. "I'll never know."

She scribbled her name at the bottom of the sheet, tore it out of the book and handed it to Maggie. "There you go."

Maggie beamed. "You're really good. Thanks, Alexandra."

"I'm glad you like it." She flipped to the next page and started on another drawing. But her mind was not on the scene before her.

Maggie had given her something to think about. She believed in her convictions; she'd had to believe. But she never thought of herself as isolated. How could she be? She had David. She had good friends, though she didn't have time to see them as much as she would like. Silly to worry about such a thing!

Maggie watched for a while. Finally, though, she looked at her watch and got to her feet. "It's almost three o'clock. I promised Morris I would get home early tonight." Maggie patted Alexandra's hand. "I hope I haven't offended you, my dear."

Alexandra could answer honestly and warmly. "No, Maggie," she said with a smile. "Of course you haven't. I didn't mean to dump my unhappy experiences on you. I've never done that before."

"I asked and I'm glad you felt comfortable enough to answer. Are you and David coming back tomorrow for the big race?"

"Yes, we'll be here."

"Good. Please tell Luke I've gone and that I'll see him early in the morning."

"I'll tell him. Goodbye, Maggie."

Chapter 5

Alexandra found Luke and David wandering among the show cars. She paused to watch for a moment. Luke had hunkered down next to a gleaming lemon yellow car, protected with velvet ropes. He was pointing to something underneath and David was nodding.

How easily and comfortably these two males, with—as far as she could tell—nothing in common, related to each other. Luke asked David a question. David answered, talking and gesturing enthusiastically. Luke's expression, as he listened, was amused.

The sunlight shone on Luke's sandy brown hair, bringing up highlights of gold and silver in the darker strands. His strong jaw was shaded by the car's shadow, giving him the look of a rogue.

Alexandra shifted her attention to the car they were discussing. The luxury automobile was sleek and low to the ground and probably built for flash, speed and glamour. It reminded her of something. She frowned, trying to remember. What—ah, yes. The car was a dead ringer for the one used in that old movie...

She approached and Luke saw her. He held her gaze for a long minute before he rose effortlessly. "Hi. Has Maggie left?"

"She said to tell you she'd see you tomorrow."

"Mom! Come see these cars. This one was in some movie." He looked to Luke for a reminder.

"The Great Gatsby," she filled in before Luke could speak.

"How did you know?"

"I saw the movie."

"Did you identify with Daisy?" asked Luke.

He was teasing. Surely he was teasing. But there had been a hint of a sneer in his tone that she didn't like. Did he think she was the naive but self-indulgent, spoiled type? She almost laughed aloud.

"I need something to drink, Mom. Why don't you get Luke to show you around? There's a car over there that belonged to Paul Newman."

He left them without a backward glance.

"See what I mean?" Alexandra set her hands on her hips and gave a resigned sigh as she watched her son disappear into the crowd. "He's determined to throw us together even though he promised me he wouldn't."

"Ignore it," Luke said shortly. He began to point out some of the more interesting cars on display. "Tomorrow they'll give out awards for various categories—" He broke off. "Are you bored?"

"Bored? No, definitely not bored." She fanned herself with her program; the weather was steamy. The temperature must have climbed into the nineties.

"You're very quiet today."

"I never have much energy when it's so hot. I would have made a good Eskimo."

He chuckled. "I thrive on hot weather."

"So does David. Is it a man thing?"

He shrugged. "Maybe. You seemed surprised when you saw me this morning."

She was hoping he wouldn't bring that up. "I was . . . surprised, almost stunned really, at how different you seem here."

"Different?"

"Yes. Of course, I've rarely seen you in anything but a formal business suit. But even when you take off your jacket, you still seem to have a rather formal personality. I don't mean to imply that there's anything wrong with that. I'm a bit formal, myself."

"I've noticed." He slid his hands into the back pockets of his jeans. "You mean I'm stuffy?"

"Well, that's a bit extreme. Here you seem more relaxed, more approachable." Like you're enjoying life instead of straining against it, she added, but only to herself. It was much too dangerous to her peace of mind for her to analyze his new persona in such an introspective way.

He had made a half turn away from her. As she looked at his profile, she realized that he wasn't pleased. "I meant it as a compliment, Luke."

"Sure," Luke said easily. His eyes had narrowed angrily at Alexandra's so-called compliment, but he was trying to hide his response from her. He supposed she'd had cause to think of him as stiff and stilted, but it was damned deflating to a man's ego when a woman judged him by his outward appearance.

Years ago when he'd gone to work for the celebrated firm, he'd wanted the job, wanted it badly enough to subdue his casual, unceremonious personality for it. He could probably ease up now; he'd more than proven himself. But the habit of being one person at work and another during his leisure hours had become ingrained.

He'd gone into the navy straight out of high school. The money he'd saved for college helped with undergraduate school, but when it came to law school, he'd wanted one of the top four. Unfortunately, the best were also the most costly. He'd graduated with a mountain of debt and a burning desire to be rich. Extraordinarily, revoltingly rich.

He'd wanted to be so rich he'd never have to do the addition in his head before writing a check. So rich he'd never have to think twice about buying a pair of shoes or concert tickets.

His childhood had been dismal, living from hand-to-mouth on whatever money he could earn doing odd jobs. He didn't remember his father, and his mother may as well have been a stranger. She provided the roof over his head and a younger sister to look after, and not much else. She was rarely at home, preferring the company of various "uncles" to his own.

The day he'd buried his mother and his little sister, he'd been sixteen. He'd stood over their graves with

tears streaming down his face, tears of resentment for
his mother, grief and regret for little six-year-old Diana. It was the age of antibiotics and drugs for every
conceivable ailment. People weren't supposed to die
from influenza.

From that time until he could escape them, he'd
lived in a series of foster homes. After straining
against the tethers and getting into trouble more times
than he cared to remember, he'd learned to adapt to
what was expected of him. Like a chameleon, he could
fit in anywhere.

Ambition had been Luke's constant companion
since that day. He'd vowed that somehow he would
escape. He would never live like that again.

He walked beside Alexandra for a few minutes before he finally responded to her comment. "The firm
I work for prefers a low profile and a fairly serious
demeanor."

"Yes, I know. My husband used to say that a lawyer had to be born into that firm."

Her words caused him to wince. "Your husband
was right. Either that or graduate in the top one per-
cent of an Ivy League school."

It was a sore point with him that, though he'd been
at the top of his class, and had gotten the job, because of his murky upbringing, he still had to play a
role for the more socially minded members of the firm
who clearly had doubts about his fitting in. Not that
he wasn't routinely serious—he'd always had to be.

And he'd paid another price. For the past ten years,
every bit of energy had been directed toward achieve-
ment. Success had been bought at the expense of per-

sonal relationships. But, he told himself, things could change now. And it had all been worth it.

He had a bank account to envy. He was building the house he'd dreamed about when he was a kid. He could afford to indulge in his favorite hobby.

Alexandra stopped in the shadow of a camera tower. She rested against the wall and resumed fanning herself.

She met his gaze and smiled, wondering where his thoughts had taken him. But inhibited as she was by his nearness, the broad shoulders, the raw masculinity he exuded, she didn't dare ask.

He propped his hand against the wall beside her head. "So I play their game. For now," he said absently as his eyes roamed over her face.

Alexandra felt a return of the breathless emotions that had so surprised her this morning. Her blood thickened in her veins, slowing down her heartbeat. His scrutiny with those hot, smoky eyes should raise blisters, but the hand that had been fanning with the program dropped to her side.

He was standing very close. She could see flecks of gold in his silver eyes. She could smell fuel and sweat and energy. But his face didn't give away an inkling of what he was thinking or feeling.

Suddenly she realized that she wanted him to kiss her.

Ridiculous. She searched through her laggard brain for something to say. "You seem to have been leading a double life, Luke. I'm amazed that I didn't see this side of you earlier."

He slanted a look at her, and this time it was quite easy to read. The look held a world of disapproval. "Perhaps you never bothered to look," he said scornfully.

She stiffened. "What does that mean?" she asked carefully.

"West Chadwick has the kind of credentials you favor. I don't. I was brought up dirt-poor, Mrs. Prescott, in coal mining country, not in country clubs. You and West are a lot alike. We both know he's the more desirable dinner date, don't we?"

She frowned, stung by his implication, even though she had taken herself to task for prejudging him, too. "That sounds like you think I'm a snob because I turned down your invitation. You don't know me well enough to make that kind of judgment."

He shrugged and levered himself away from the wall. He took a couple of steps and halted with his back to her. "Sorry."

He didn't sound sorry. He sounded as though he didn't give a damn. Well, that was just fine with her. She wanted to leave, to get out of here. Now. She felt stifled, suffocated, disappointed. Deeply disappointed. But she couldn't leave.

"If you'd like to get back to town, I can bring David home when the show's over."

Had he read her mind? She looked up.

And was caught in those steely gray eyes. Glacial, chilling, they seemed to stab at her.

"Luke, I—" She broke off and shook her head helplessly. "I've said something to insult you. Though I'm not sure what it was, I'm sorry for it." She didn't make the mistake of meeting his eyes again. Instead, she resolutely kept her gaze lower.

On his mouth. But that was another mistake. Even thinned in anger, his lips were amazingly sensual. "The heat is giving me a headache. If you're sure you don't mind—"

"Not at all. Wait here and I'll get David. We'll walk you to your car." He strode in the direction of the refreshment stand as though glad to escape.

She wanted to stop him, to say no. She wanted to leave right now. But she waited.

When Luke returned with David, the boy looked at her worriedly. "Mom, are you sick?"

"No, honey. Not sick. But Luke offered to bring you home. And you know how I hate the heat..." Her voice trailed off. "If it's okay with you."

Luke stood with his hand on David's shoulder and watched as Alexandra drove away.

"Was Mom mad about something?" David asked.

"Not at you," Luke said with a deep sigh. Why had he acted like such a horse's ass? "Me. I'm afraid I said something that offended her."

David looked surprised. "About what?"

"I think I was—" Jealous?

"Jealous?" said David with a grin.

Surprised by the boy's insight, Luke kept quiet. They turned and headed back toward the grid.

"You know," David said after they'd gone a short distance, "my mom has changed a lot since my dad died. She never used to be so serious. She used to laugh all the time. She was a lot of fun."

Luke almost smiled. The kid was trying to sell him on Alexandra. He made an effort to take the same advice he'd given to her—ignore it. "After your dad died, I imagine she had to be serious, didn't she?"

"Yes, sir, she did. She's worked hard."

"And been successful." The compliment was a mistake; it put the hopeful gleam back in David's eye.

"I'll bet Mr. Chadwick turned her against you. He'd do something like that. He doesn't like you much."

Luke wasn't sure how to answer. "He likes your mom." He didn't elaborate; the details of Chadwick's plans for seduction weren't for David's ears.

"You like her, too, don't you?"

"Yes, I do. But he and your mother have known each other longer."

"He may like her, but he sure doesn't like kids. He thinks they get in his way." David's mouth took on a stubborn look. "He also thinks I'm so dumb, I don't know what he's up to."

"Ah, what is that?" Luke asked.

"He wants to get her into bed, of course. Honestly, Luke, I'm fourteen, not four."

"Yeah." Luke sighed. "Kids today *do* grow up too quickly."

"Aw, c'mon, Luke. You sound just like Mom. I thought you were different."

"I thought so, too. Obviously I was wrong," Luke said almost to himself. "Anyway, Mr. Chadwick, like you, is an only child. He probably was not around many younger kids when he was growing up. Maybe he just doesn't know how to relate to you." Luke didn't know why he was explaining Chadwick to this boy.

"Were you? An only child?"

Suddenly, Luke felt the blood drain from his face. "No," he said more harshly than he'd meant. But his harshness had the desired effect.

David looked astonished, but he changed the subject.

Alexandra was glad to be home. Alone. The sun had gone down but darkness had brought no relief from the enervating heat. Her feet felt like lead and her head like a water balloon. And her heart—her heart felt unprotected, exposed.

She had just inserted her key in the front door, when a voice startled her. "Hey, Alexandra, the police want you to call them as soon as possible." West ambled out of his door and across the porch to where she was standing.

She stopped and studied his tall form for a moment. He moved easily, fluidly. His well-defined muscles were displayed to perfection in a pair of jeans and a white T-shirt. His smile was gorgeous, he exuded sensuality the way other people sweat...and, to her disgust, he left her unmoved.

He was a nice man. He had a good sense of humor and a good mind. So what was wrong with her?

"Oh, damn," she groaned under her breath, then smiled at him in apology. "It's too hot to deal with those people."

"Yeah. And it's Saturday night, too," he went on with a grin. "The officer said you had his number. I thought you might appreciate some moral support."

"No date tonight? You must be slipping, West." She lifted her damp hair off her neck. "Thanks. I'll call him right now. Give me five minutes to splash water on my face and I'll fix us something cold to drink."

Fifteen minutes later, she and West relaxed in her living room with tall glasses of ice tea. She had pulled her hair off her neck in a tortoiseshell clasp and changed her sneakers for sandals. A shower would help even more—the shorts she had donned this morning were a wrinkled mess and the crisp white shirt was now damp and limp from the humidity. But the officer had said he would be right over.

"Where's David?" West asked.

"He's with Luke," she answered absently. She closed her eyes and rubbed the cold glass across her forehead. "I feel almost human again. Are you hungry? I could probably find the energy to fix sandwiches."

When he didn't answer, she opened her eyes to find him gazing at her with the unmistakable gleam of desire. She frowned and he recovered almost immediately.

"Why don't we wait until the police finish, then order Chinese?" he said smoothly.

The doorbell rang and she got to her feet. "That sounds even better." The officer who had worked on her burglary case was at the door, accompanied by two other men. He introduced one as his lieutenant.

The other man removed his hat, then introduced himself. He took a leather folder from his inside breast pocket and deftly flipped it open to show them his identification. "Mrs. Prescott, Mr. Chadwick. I am Special Agent Ash Zarcone with the FBI."

The FBI? What was going on? Despite the heat outside, the agent's collar was perfectly smooth, his tie perfectly knotted and his dark suit undefeated by the humidity. How did he remain so crisp? she wondered. And the hat—in the South, a man wearing a dress hat was a rare sight; she hadn't seen one in a long time.

As always when she was faced with someone colorful or intriguing, her fingers itched for a pencil.

"May we sit down?" he asked.

"Of course." She returned to her seat on the sofa, which was a mistake. The agent placed his hat on the coffee table and sat in a chair to her right. His head was above hers, looking down. Their positions made her uncomfortable. "Would anyone like a glass of ice tea?" she asked.

The younger officer, who had remained on his feet, looked as if he wanted to accept but the FBI agent spoke for them all. "No, thank you, Mrs. Prescott. This won't take long."

The older policeman seemed to make a decision. "You don't need us, Zarcone. We need to get back— we're on duty," he said.

The agent nodded his dismissal. "Thanks. I'll see you at the station later."

The police officers left and Alexandra waited for the FBI agent to explain why he was here.

"Mrs. Prescott, it is routine for local police to forward unidentified fingerprints to FBI headquarters. A print found during the investigation of the break-in of your condo was in our files. The print belongs to a man named Ned Austin."

He paused, smiling tightly, perhaps waiting for a reaction. "The name isn't familiar," she said.

His smile went askew. "I didn't really think it would be. We apprehended Austin a number of years ago. He was sentenced to prison, served some time and was released on parole last year." He took a folder from his briefcase, extracted a picture from the folder and handed it to her. "The parole officer assigned to his case hasn't heard from Austin since January."

She looked at the face, then shook her head; she had never seen the man. "I don't know him. I'm sorry I can't help you." She handed the picture back but he didn't put it away. Instead, he dropped it on the coffee table.

"Austin was originally convicted of smuggling technological data—computer chips, to be exact. The fact that his fingerprint has shown up here, in your condo, is a puzzle. But we can't help speculating that he may have a connection to a smuggling ring we're investigating here. Again, the smuggled goods are computer chips. We believe the ring is tied in to the murder of the pilot at the airport last month."

The murder had been highly publicized and she remembered reading that the FBI had been called in. "I was at the airport that day."

West, who slouched comfortably with his ankles crossed and his fingers linked over his stomach, sat up abruptly. "You were?"

Zarcone leaned forward, suddenly alert. She could see the excitement in his eyes. "The day the pilot was murdered?" the agent said.

She nodded. "To meet David's plane," she said to West. She explained to Zarcone, "My son had been visiting his grandparents in Switzerland."

"Did you see anything at all that might have aroused your suspicions?"

Alexandra shook her head. "No, nothing." The telephone rang. She excused herself and reached across the back of the sofa to answer. "Hello."

Silence. She gripped the receiver until her knuckles were white and forced her breathing to remain steady and rhythmic. Then, at last, she heard the dial tone.

"They hung up," she explained, glad that Zarcone hadn't seemed to notice anything amiss. "Now, what were you asking?"

"The Atlanta police tell me that you are an artist and some sketchbooks were taken during the robbery."

"That's right. I didn't understand why."

"Do you ever draw in public?"

"Of course. I was drawing the day of the murder. I have a picture of the pilot who was killed. But not of this man," she said, indicating the picture on the table.

"Mrs. Prescott, I want you to take me through that day, step-by-step." The agent leaned back in his chair.

"If the offer's still open, I would like a glass of ice tea."

West stopped her when she started to rise. She wondered why he was frowning so, why he seemed so distracted. "I'll get it," he said.

Alexandra sipped her own tea and replayed the scene in the airport. "The planes were late that day because of the weather—all of them—and the lounge was crowded. I waited for almost an hour. I didn't mind waiting, except that I was looking forward to David's homecoming. Anyway, there were a lot of interesting people so I found myself a corner and sketched."

"And some of your sketchbooks were taken during the burglary."

"Yes."

"I wonder," said the agent. "I didn't mean to interrupt. Please go on."

She spread her hands. "That's all. I drew until they announced the flight." Her eyebrows furrowed.

"What?" said Zarcone. "You look as if you remembered something?"

She did, she remembered the feeling she'd had that someone was watching... West reappeared with the glass of tea for Zarcone. "Oh, I ran into one of your clients that day, West," she said.

"One of my clients?"

At that moment, the front door opened. David and Luke came in. Alexandra met Luke's gaze, then quickly looked away. During the explanations and introductions, she could almost feel the agent's impatience.

"You were about to tell us about seeing a client of Mr. Chadwick's," he prompted.

David had disappeared toward his room and Luke sat in one of the chairs opposite Alexandra's spot on the sofa. "One of the firm's clients?" he asked.

She ignored him. "You introduced me to Paul Henderson, didn't you, West?"

"That's right. You went with me to the summer party the firm gives each year. Henderson was there."

He was talking to her but his gaze was fixed on Luke, who had stiffened at the mention of the name. What was going on here? Had the burglars been looking for him or Chadwick? Had they broken into the wrong condo? He met West's gaze, his eyebrow raised in inquiry.

"Later," West mouthed.

Obviously whatever was relevant here had been said before he and David arrived. He settled back to listen.

Alexandra was grateful for the opportunity to clear up one misunderstanding right now. For some reason, she found it intolerable that Luke would think her a liar as well as a snob. "Your date for the summer party couldn't make it and you asked me to fill in at the last minute," she said to West while looking at Luke.

"First time I've ever been happy to be stood up," West said cheerfully.

Luke's expression remained skeptical. She wondered why she had bothered.

Zarcone shook his head. "I can't see the connection, if there is one. Did you draw a picture of this man?"

"I'm almost positive I didn't, but I can check."

Again she had his full attention. "I thought all your sketchbooks were stolen," the agent said.

"Not the latest one. I always carry it in my bag. I'll get it."

She was back in moments with the book. She leafed through it, folding back the ends to leave eight or ten pages free and handed the book to Zarcone. "These are the drawings I did that day."

The agent riffled through them. The other two men moved to stand behind his chair. "Are they realistic?" Zarcone asked. "I mean, is this how the people look?"

"Yes," she answered.

"Is what's-his-name—Henderson—among these drawings?"

"No, I'm almost sure he isn't." She took the book for a minute and thumbed through it. Henderson wasn't there. "No, I remember now, he didn't come in until after I stopped drawing." She handed the book to the agent.

Zarcone sighed. "There doesn't seem to be anything helpful here."

Luke froze. "Back up," he said sharply. "Let me see that last picture."

"This one? It's a kid," the agent said. "Do you know him?"

"No. My mistake."

West had moved up to examine the sketch, close enough for Luke to grab his arm and squeeze a warning. They exchanged looks. Luke shook his head, a slight movement, not detectable by the others. West understood.

The sketch was of a child tugging at a uniform sleeve with four gold stripes. It wasn't the child that interested either of them. It was the hand at the end of the sleeve—and the ring on the hand. The ring was very distinctive. And they both knew who it belonged to.

"May I take the book with me?" Zarcone asked Alexandra. "A drawing isn't the documentation that a photograph would be, but the sketches might be useful."

She hesitated. The sketches she'd made today at Road Atlanta were also in that book. She'd been toying with the idea of doing something with them for David's room.

Bosh! Who was she trying to fool? Herself? The drawings she'd done of Luke were in there, too. And they were most revealing.

Zarcone must have misunderstood her hesitation. "I'll make copies and return your book tomorrow."

"That wasn't— Of course, you may take the book."

He reached inside his coat and came out with a card and a pen. "I'm putting a number on the back here. I can be reached at any time. Please call me if you think of anything else that happened that day, even if you don't think it's relevant. I'm not sure we know what *is* relevant about all this. But it seems your break-in might have been more than a robbery. I'm not trying to frighten you, but I want you to be aware of the situation."

He scribbled as he spoke. She took the card. "Thank you, Mr. Zarcone."

He retrieved his hat, she walked him to the door and said good-night. West and Luke were right behind her when she turned.

"I'll be going," said West. "See you later, Alexandra."

"I'll walk out with you," said Luke.

Alexandra hid her surprise. The two men were actually being polite to each other. And before the police had come, West appeared to have settled in for the evening. What happened to ordering Chinese?

Luke must have misread the surprise on her face. He glanced at the door; West had disappeared. "Will you be all right?" he asked quietly.

If she wouldn't be, she would never let him know it. "I'll be fine."

"I apologize for the things I said earlier. I was pretty rough on you." He raked his fingers through his rumpled hair. A gesture of frustration? she wondered. "I hope it won't cause you to decide to skip the race tomorrow."

"Of course not." She lifted her chin. He was still looking at her with those skeptical gray eyes. "Even if I wanted to, David wouldn't hear of it," she said truthfully. "You know that."

"Yes, but *you* know that I'd make sure he got there and back."

And I'd have to explain why. She remembered the happiness on the boy's face as the silver car streaked across the finish line this morning. Anyone who could put that expression on David's face deserved her admiration and appreciation, not her anger.

Yet, he'd insulted her and she just couldn't let it slide by. "I'll take him."

"Okay. See you tomorrow."

"What was said before I came in?" Luke asked. They were standing at the porch rail, and they both kept their voices low.

"The FBI thinks the pilot's murder is related to a smuggling ring operating out of Atlanta. A print found in Alexandra's condo has been identified as belonging to one Ned Austin, convicted of smuggling, now out on parole."

"Drugs?"

"No. Computer technology. What do you think?" asked West.

"I think there are a hell of a lot of coincidences here. And I know we've both seen that ring before. The one on the pilot's hand in the drawing of the child." The ring was fashioned using a computer chip in a setting the way someone else would use a precious stone. Encircling the chip were a series of zeros and ones, computer language for the company of the wearer.

"And the man who designed the ring for himself and brags that he never takes it off was at the airport, but is no pilot," Luke finished.

West sighed heavily and massaged the back of his neck. "Yeah. But what the hell was Henderson doing in a pilot's uniform?"

Luke looked at West keenly. "Do you think she could have made a mistake?"

"No. I've seen a lot of her work. The characters are done with a minimum of fussiness but the details are perfect. She notices everything."

Luke was inclined to agree. "But maybe she noticed the ring on Henderson's hand and added it to the pilot's."

West shook his head. "She said Henderson didn't come in while she was drawing."

"And there's the matter of the computer connection," Luke added.

Henderson, the client who was driving them both crazy to get his operation moved offshore as quickly as possible, was the owner of a small but very successful computer business, which specialized in the latest advanced technology for the much-touted information highway of tomorrow.

"It's too much of a coincidence, isn't it?" he said heavily.

"I'm afraid so," West agreed.

Their gazes met and for once there was not a trace of hostility between them. Instead, there was complete understanding of the quandary they faced.

Lawyer-client confidentiality was inviolate. If they knew for a fact that Henderson had committed a crime, they could not turn him in.

If, however, they knew a crime was going to be committed in the future—a pending crime—they were morally obligated to report it.

"God, this is every lawyer's nightmare. Do we really have information relating to a pending crime? Or are we just naturally suspicious?"

"Well, we can't blow the whistle on Henderson for anything he's done in the past."

"No, but we sure as hell can ask him a few questions on our own."

"We'll have to tread very lightly. Make an appointment. Face him together."

"Yeah. Come on. We'll call him right now from my place."

"Luke." West grinned for the first time since they'd seen the drawing.

"What?" Luke snapped. He was already reaching for his keys.

"It's eleven o'clock. It's Labor Day weekend. Even if he's home, this isn't the way to begin."

"Either now or at 7:00 a.m. tomorrow. I can't hang around here any later. I have something to do."

"You racing tomorrow?"

Luke rammed the key home, and the door swung inward. "Yeah. Did Alexandra tell you?"

"No, I asked the condo manager about the trailer that was parked in the lot. I looked under the tarp, too. Good-looking car."

"Thanks."

The following morning, Luke called the home number of the client. A man answered, introduced himself as the majordomo and informed Luke that

Mr. and Mrs. Henderson were away for the weekend. They would return on Tuesday.

Luke cursed and punched in West's number. "He's out of town. He'll be back Tuesday."

"Figures," West answered. "I'll try his office voice mail later, on the off chance he keeps in touch even on holidays. But we'll probably have to make an appointment on Tuesday morning. At least the man won't try to avoid his lawyers."

"Chadwick?"

"What?"

Luke took a deep breath. He hated like hell to ask this man for anything. "Shall we put our rivalry on the back burner until this is resolved?"

West hesitated for a minute. Then Luke could hear him chuckle. "Definitely," he said at last.

Chapter 6

An air of expectancy stirred the noisy crowd, sharpening laughter, raising voices. This was the last race of the day, of the vintage racing event for this year.

The temperature was cooler than yesterday's had been, but not much. Luke had to be sweltering under all those layers of clothing. But he didn't look hot and uncomfortable. He looked composed and controlled.

And large, very large.

He wore an insulated burgundy jumpsuit with silver racing stripes. Before he pulled the zipper closed over his chest, Alexandra had gotten a glimpse of dark, curling hair beneath the fire-protective undersuit. He would also wear a hood, similar to a ski mask, of the same safety fabric. Earlier, he'd answered David's questions, explaining that wearing the protective clothing was a rule of the racing federation.

Despite his repeated reassurances that vintage racers were primarily hobbyists, however, Alexandra understood that when men and machines were combined at high speeds there was always an element of danger. After watching the races today, she was certain of it. But she was also sure that this man knew what he was doing.

As she and David watched, Luke assembled and checked his equipment, inspected the car one last time, conferred with Maggie. Nothing was left to chance.

He took a long drink from a bottle of water, wiping his mouth with the back of his hand. "David, would you get my safety hood and helmet, please?"

"Sure, Luke." Her son gave her a conspiratorial look and took off at a run.

"I'm...uh...going to verify the fuel mix," said Maggie, moving off.

They were alone—or as alone as they could be among thousands of people—for the first time today. The side of a large tractor-trailer truck concealed them from the body of the crowd.

They had been painfully polite to each other all day. He hadn't forgiven her for her remarks yesterday, but he was no longer angry. However, it had fallen to David, Maggie and Maggie's husband, Morris, who had come along for the final races, to keep any conversation going.

Alexandra crossed her arms over her chest and watched, while she waited for him to make a point.

Luke glanced at her and away. He replaced the cap on the water bottle and stored it in one of the many pockets in his suit. "Was that maneuver too obvious?"

She dropped her eyes to her toes and smiled slightly. "I'd say so, yes."

"How about a kiss for luck?" Luke asked casually as he reached in his back pocket for his insulated gauntlets.

Alexandra gaped at him, but she covered quickly. He seemed to be engrossed with the long gloves.

Had she been forgiven, after all, for yesterday's awkward observations about his double life?

And had *she* forgiven *him* for thinking her a snob?

She took a breath, suddenly wary of the idea of his lips touching hers. "Do you think it will help you win the race?" she asked his unreadable profile.

He turned his head to look at her and grinned. "Couldn't hurt."

"I'm not so sure about that," she murmured. The noise of the engines had drowned out the sound of her soft words, but it didn't matter. He was focused on her lips and he understood.

For a moment, she was beguiled by the contrast between his strong white teeth and his tanned skin. His gray eyes, which could be as cold as steel, were warm and smoky. An answering smile spread across her face.

He made no sudden moves, but neither did he reduce the intensity of his gaze. When his hands settled on her shoulders, she didn't protest.

One corner of his mouth lifted and his head blotted out the sun as he slowly brought her closer and bent to her. His mouth was gentle at first, but when she didn't pull away, a spark from somewhere inside her caught fire and immediately became a conflagration.

Alexandra had not been kissed in four years.

She had not felt a man's hard body next to her softer one, a man's hands holding her. She'd forgotten how wonderful, how luxurious an amorous touch felt.

His lips were firm and hungry. His tongue traced her mouth, appealing for entry. With a soft moan, she wrapped her arms around Luke's waist and parted her lips. His tongue delved inside, giving her an enticing, erotic taste of him.

The substance of his muscle and bone, of his rushing blood and beating heart, evoked a response on some deep emotional level that wiped out their surroundings completely. Now she knew why human beings withered and died when deprived of physical contact with another.

Perhaps she would have reacted this way with anyone, but she didn't think so. This man, this day, this time—she had avoided him, yet on some subconscious level, she'd yearned for him, too. Like a thirst for water, a hunger for food, there was this urgency, which would not be denied any longer.

His suit was slick under her hands and she held on to him as though she would float away if not anchored.

Luke gathered Alexandra close. One hand slid to cup her head, adjusting the angle for his kiss. God, she felt so good against him. So curvy and feminine, and yet so strong. "Your mouth," he murmured against her lips. "It's so sweet...like your voice, like honey." Her breath came out on a sigh that mingled with his.

He backed against the fender of his car and drew her into more intimate contact, bringing her curves into flawless alignment with his own angles. His sex measured the angle between her thighs and found a perfect fit. The pleasure of being there was overwhelming.

He withdrew from the kiss slowly, carefully, but he kept her in his arms against him. "Allie," he breathed into her soft hair. "Alexandra, I want you," he said huskily. "I've wanted you for a long, long time."

"Yes, oh, yes," she answered.

A bark of raucous laughter suddenly jolted him out of the haze of desire. Over her head, he squeezed his eyes shut, struggling to reestablish his equilibrium, fighting the haze that surrounded them.

She tilted her head back, and he was almost lost again. Her emerald eyes had the same dazed, unsteady look. "For so long, I haven't even thought about..." She faltered, then went on. "About being touched and held for so long." She shook her head as though to clear it.

He held her and watched. Slowly those beautiful eyes cleared; she rallied. Her enchanting expression of confusion turned to bewilderment, then to horror.

"Omigosh." She would have jerked free of his arms if he had allowed it. She peered over her shoulder to see if anyone had come near.

He could have told her that they had indeed been seen, not only by Maggie, but also by David, who had come around the corner of the truck, then withdrawn. But he decided, with a wry twist of his mouth, that discretion was the better part of valor.

He reached out to brush a tangle of hair back from her face. "Lady, you do pack a powerful punch. And I meant it when I said I want you."

Her eyes grew wide, so wide he felt he could drown in them. "I can't," she said. Her voice was husky, too, and he thought he heard a pang of regret there.

"Why not?" he asked tenderly. "Don't tell me you don't feel as stirred up as I do, because I won't believe it."

"No, I mean yes, I do." She stepped out of his arms. Her heat-flushed face was damp. She breathed deeply, held the breath for a second, then let it out.

"Do I hear a 'but' in there somewhere?" Luke held himself motionless, waiting.

"Yes. *But* I have a teenage son, Luke. I know that wouldn't stop a lot of people but it stops me."

He gazed deep into her eyes, awed and amazed. A smile, not wholly humorous, twisted his mouth; he laughed under his breath. "I understand," he said. Then, in an attempt to lighten the atmosphere, he added, "I sure as hell don't want to, but I do."

"Thank you."

He slapped his hands together and looked around. "Now, where are David and Maggie? If I have the luck that kiss promised, I'll win this race for sure."

"Your race! Oh, dear, Luke, you shouldn't have been distracted—"

Her statement was severed by his laughter; deep and heartfelt, the sound of it was remarkable. She had wondered if Luke ever just let go like this. Now she had her answer.

She stared at him as he threw his head back. A smile began to grow on her face and soon she joined him, their laughter mingling in the warm September air. Over the noise of the crowds and the engines, she thought it made a breathtaking duet.

"What's so funny?" said David as he appeared from behind them. Maggie was not far behind.

Luke chuckled and Alexandra saw the knowing smile on her son's face, but for the moment, she didn't care if they had been seen. That kiss had been worth all the explanations she would have to make. A feeling of euphoria lifted her spirits and she let herself soar with it.

When the laughter was finally spent, Alexandra continued to grin at him. "I've never heard you laugh like that," she said.

His smile faded, replaced by an expression of thoughtfulness. "I should do it more often, shouldn't I?"

"Time to go," Maggie said.

"Yeah, I'm ready." Luke pulled at the gauntlets he'd dropped when he'd reached for her. He took the safety hood and helmet from David and fitted both over his head, but he paused, letting the chin strap dangle free for a minute. He looked at her. "Would you and David like to go to the windup party after the races? It's usually fun."

Alexandra wanted to keep this day alive for a few hours more, and yet she hesitated. "I don't know, Luke. Tomorrow's a school day for David."

He kept her gaze captive with his hot gray eyes. "We don't have to stay late."

"Okay. We'd like that."

David had chosen to watch the race from the grid with Maggie and her husband; he seemed to relish feeling in the center of things. And besides, he'd informed her importantly, "Everyone watches the race from down here, Mom."

But the noisy, frantic atmosphere was beginning to frazzle Alexandra's enjoyment of the event. She remembered the dramatic view of the rolling hills and trees as a backdrop for the race. She told David where she was going and hurried to the tower overlooking the finish line.

She climbed the stairs to find the party in high gear. The area was twice as crowded as yesterday and the noise level seemed to have quadrupled. Several people she'd met during the past two days called out greetings, one party asked her to join them, but she wanted to be alone, to think about what had just happened.

The race cars were already moving down the track behind the pace car by the time Alexandra made her way to the window. She saw Luke's car right away and fixed on the silver hood as the pace car peeled off and the racers accelerated. Rounding the first turn, out of sight behind the trees, Luke was in the middle of the pack.

It took several minutes before the cars appeared from behind another copse of trees at the opposite side of the track. Luke seemed to have moved up toward the front, but she couldn't be sure.

She stood in her corner and watched the cars go around and around. Luke moved up a car or two after each lap, until the flag signaling the final lap was waved. He was vying with a midnight black racer—she didn't know the model—as the drivers sped by and disappeared behind the trees for the last time.

Alexandra held her breath and crossed her fingers, and kept her gaze glued to the spot where the cars would pass, headed for the finish line and the checkered flag.

At the very last minute, Luke nosed past the black car to win the race.

Luke felt the rush of exhilaration as he nosed the small car into the grid and brought it to a halt. He yanked off the helmet and the safety hood. His hair was plastered to his head and he finger-combed some of the sweat away. Well-wishers surrounded the car and he responded to the backslapping compliments, the cheers, the applause.

But the first person he really focused on was Maggie. There was a smile on her face and moisture in her eyes. Their mutual grins said more than words what the win had meant to them both.

Crossing a finish line before anyone else wasn't the point. The shared accomplishment was. And their symbolic journey from the coalfields of West Virginia. He climbed out of the car and hugged her hard.

David was with her. The boy's face was in danger of splitting wide open. His voice, which was beginning to change, was high and shrill with excitement. "Luke! Luke! It was great!"

Luke hugged him, too. And met his hand in a high-five slap. "It *was* great, the greatest. I did it! I actually did it!"

He looked around but didn't see Alexandra. He knew a moment's disappointment, then assumed that she'd watched from the tower. She would be here in a minute.

David's excitement could not be contained. Amid the commotion and the crowd, he danced and hopped and swayed, laughing.

Even as Luke accepted congratulations and talked to the people who stopped, he smiled at David's unrestrained exuberance. Smiled fondly. And lovingly.

This kid was getting to him. So was the kid's mother.

At last the excitement began to ebb; the people around them began to move away. But there was still no sign of Alexandra. Luke craned his neck, looking over the heads of the crowd between their position and the tower atop the hill.

Finally, he took David aside. "I'm going to look for your mother. She may not be able to find us in this pack of people. I'll be back in a minute."

"Okay," said David.

The tower erupted into cheers after Luke crossed the finish line. Alexandra had been seen with Luke so she was the recipient of all the cheers, all the back-slapping, all the laughing congratulations.

"You're with Luke Quinlan, aren't you? Tell him Kay and Bill said good job." She nodded.

"Tell Luke that Homer Wilkins will be out to get him next year."

"Okay." She smiled at Homer and edged toward the tower steps.

And from a beautiful young woman with a low breathy voice, "Tell Luke that Angela said hi."

It took her a while to get free. Out of breath, she finally left the tower and hurried toward the grid. She waded into the crowd, trying to see David or Maggie or Luke, but there were simply too many people. Some were already loading the classic vehicles into trucks or onto trailers, but most were merely enjoying the end of the event, saying goodbye to friends they wouldn't see for a while. Having a last toast.

Finally, in exasperation, she headed back toward the hill overlooking the grid. She would be able to see all the area from there.

When she got to the top, she shielded her eyes from the brilliant sun and swept her gaze over the grid below. At last she spotted Luke. He was taller than most of the people around him, and he seemed to be searching the area, too.

She started to lift her hand, to wave in hopes of attracting his attention, when all at once, without warning, something dark and hot came down over her head, blotting out all sounds and sight. She was lifted off her feet.

Alexandra erupted, screaming and flailing her arms, but her screams were stifled by the heavy cloth and her struggles were ineffective. Whoever carried her was strong. Frantic, she continued to struggle.

How could this be happening with so many people around? But the people on the grid were caught up in the excitement of the just-completed race. They weren't paying attention to the area atop the hill.

"Shut up, bitch," said a muffled male voice. He was moving fast. Really fast. Where was he taking her? She remembered, with a black premonition, a row of deserted garages off to one side near the fence. Oh, God, was the monster going to rape her? Or kill her?

No! She wouldn't have it! He was carrying her over his arms, like a heavy coat. She kicked backward and made contact with something. She heard him curse. Yes! Then his arms contracted painfully around her until she was afraid her ribs would crack. Her breathing was cut off by the force and her head began to swim.

Suddenly, she was dropped onto a hard surface. Her elbow hit pavement, sending pain up her arm and bringing tears to her eyes. A heavy weight was across her chest, rendering her helpless. With her uninjured arm, she pushed against the fabric but he was holding it down, too.

"Listen up, bitch. You're going to keep your mouth shut about what you saw at the airport. You're going to do that because we're taking your son. You're going to convince the police to drop the investigation long enough for certain people to get out of town. You do what we tell you and he won't be hurt."

Alexandra had become still at his words.

David! Oh, dear God, there were more than one of them, and they had David! She couldn't bear it!

Beneath the heavy fabric she started to nod furiously. "Yes, yes, anything. Don't hurt him. Please, for the love of God, don't hurt him!" She was crying, sobbing. "I'll do whatever you say. Please. Please."

"Remember, stall this investigation for at least a week."

The weight was suddenly removed. She lay there for a second, confused by its loss. Then she heard a sharp rumbling sound, followed by another click—metal on metal. She fought her way free of the heavy blanket and rolled to her knees, dragging in great gulps of air. The room spun around her. She breathed carefully to fight off nausea.

As she had feared, she was in an abandoned garage. Debris of one kind or another had gathered in dark, filthy corners, along with the deserted webs of long-dead spiders. A buildup of grease on the exposed concrete floors had acted as a magnet to dirt and dust. The width of the garage at one end was a huge door on tracks that curved to the ceiling. The only illumination came through grimy panes across the top of the roll-up door, and that light was dim and murky. The only sounds that reached her ears were distant and unidentifiable.

When her head stopped spinning, she struggled to her feet and stumbled in that direction. She had to get out of here; she had to find her son. She curved her fingers under the bottom of the door and strained to raise it. But it wouldn't budge. Locked. The effort renewed the throbbing pain in her elbow.

David.

"David!" she screamed, her desperate voice echoing in the empty chamber. She slapped at the panels, with the flat of her hand, with her fist, with her forehead. Tears were streaming down her cheeks. "Dear God, you wouldn't do this to me again, would you?" she whimpered. "Please don't do this again."

She finally realized that no one could hear her. No one.

Defeated, she slid slowly to her knees.

How long had she been locked in here? Seconds? Minutes? Luke would look for her. Maggie would miss her. Someone would get her out eventually. But David would be far away by then.

"Think, Alexandra." Her eyes darted frantically into the dark corners of the empty chamber. She got to her feet again, holding her injured elbow, and began a systematic search around the walls. She kicked at a pile of debris. A beer can rolled away from a used condom, and dust clouded around her knees.

She wrinkled her nose in disgust, but she kept searching. Finally, she saw something rusty in a back corner, something metal, sticking out from under the deteriorated carcass of an animal. She kicked the animal off the object. There at her feet was a wrench minus its bottom jaw. She pounced on the broken tool as though it were made of gold and ran back to the door.

If she could break one of the windowpanes, maybe she could make someone hear her. She stretched high, as high as she could reach, drew her good arm back and struck hard. The pane of glass shattered, raining sharp fragments down on her, and the wrench went flying through the window.

"Help! Help me!" She was yelling before she heard the tool hit the pavement outside. "Help! Luke! Get me out of here!" She screamed for what seemed like hours before she finally heard someone calling her name. "I'm here!" she called back.

"Alexandra!" It was Luke and his voice was rough. "Thank God."

She heard the fear in his voice, as well. "Yes, I'm here! I'm locked in." And despite herself, she began to cry.

"Don't cry, baby. I'll have you out of there in a minute."

"Hurry, Luke. Please hurry," she said, sobbing.

The screech of metal, a sharp crack, and then the door was rising, letting in the brilliant sunlight, fresh air and Luke. He still wore the racing suit. Dusty, sweaty, tired and worried, he was balance in a world turned upside down.

She raced into his arms and they closed around her like a vise.

"Alexandra, my God, what in hell happened?" Gently he pushed her back, dusted the glass out of her hair, cradled her face. His hands were shaking.

"A man. He had a blanket or something. He grabbed me...." Her voice broke. "He has—"

Luke's face had drained of color. A muscle in his jaw jumped spasmodically. Again, he hauled her against him, his big hands moving over her back in a comforting stroke. "Did he—hurt you?"

She was shaking her head before he finished. She tried to pull away. "No, no. But he said he has David! He said—"

Luke's eyes narrowed as he brought her back into the circle of his arms, more tenderly this time. "I just left David. He's fine."

Her face turned up to him, hope warring in her eyes with disbelief.

"David is fine," he repeated. "Come on, I'll show you." He kept her within the circle of his arm as he headed toward the grid area. "Can you walk all right?"

"Yes," she said, but she sagged against him, glad of his support. The action pinned her injured arm between them. She pulled back with an involuntary gasp. The pain shot up her arm again, along her shoulder.

He stopped. "What is it?"

"My elbow. I hit it on the concrete floor. It's all right, let's go."

Luke moved to Alexandra's other side and dropped his arm to her waist instead of her shoulder. His mouth twisted agonizingly as he looked down at her. Not only her arm but her knees were scraped. Her face was smeared with dirt and grease. And her eyes—the expression of terror in her wonderful eyes, and his inability to erase it, hurt him more than he'd ever believed he could be hurt.

At that moment, Luke realized that strong feelings were brewing in him for this woman, much stronger than straightforward desire. He wanted to pick her up and carry her away—away from all fear, all worry, all pain.

He wasn't ready for feelings like that, he reminded himself. Despite the kiss they'd shared before the race, despite the heat, the passion, the excitement of that moment, he wasn't ready.

Maggie had warned him this morning of Alexandra's obsessive need for independence. She had a lot of emotional baggage relating to her dead husband—not to mention a teenage son.

Whom he had to locate right now. To relieve her mind and his.

They finally arrived at Maggie's van. David was nowhere to be seen. "Where's David?" said Luke tightly.

Maggie was packing away her tools. She glanced around. "He was here just a minute ago. He probably went to get a cold drink."

Alexandra put her hand to her heart. "Oh, no."

"What's wrong?" asked Maggie. For the first time, she noticed Alexandra's appearance. "What on earth happened to you?"

Alexandra brushed her hair off her face distractedly. "I don't have time to explain now, Maggie. I've got to find David."

"He couldn't have gone far. Come on, I'll help you look," Maggie said, slamming the door to the van. She called to Morris, who came hurrying over.

"What's up?" he asked. Maggie explained quickly.

"We'll find him," he said to Alexandra.

Luke had been studying the area, but his arm remained around Alexandra.

She pulled away from him, fully aware of what he was about to say. "Thanks, Maggie, Morris."

Luke tried for patience. "Alexandra, you wait here. I'll find David and bring him to you."

Luke didn't notice the look Alexandra gave him. She wasn't going to sit idly by while her son was missing. He didn't know her very well, if he'd thought she would. "No," she said firmly.

God, she was a stubborn woman. "Hang on a minute. You're not going off alone. Maggie, you stay with Alexandra. Search from here to the track. I'll get a security guard to help us and search the area toward the fence. Morris, you cover the grid. Ask people if they've seen him. He's made a lot of friends this weekend. If you see or hear anything, sing out."

Luke strode off in the direction of the fence, which was comparatively deserted. If David had been taken, his abductors would try to get the boy as far away from people as quickly as possible. He spotted a security guard he knew.

He hurriedly enlisted the guard's help and they started off in opposite directions.

Luke had gone just a few dozen yards when he saw something that made his blood chill. About forty yards away, near the fence, two men appeared to be wrestling next to the open door of a dark van. Navy blue or black.

One man grabbed his shin, stepping aside long enough for Luke to catch sight of a third figure. The tableau included a boy, struggling. A boy in a red shirt exactly like David's.

"Hey! This way!" Luke yelled to the guard. He set off like a shot, sprinting in the van's direction. "You, there. Let that boy go."

One of the men whirled, saw the big man coming and jumped into the driver's seat. He slammed the door and got the van in gear, yelling at his accomplice. The other man, who still had a hold on the struggling David, looked up. He gave the boy a shove and vaulted into the van's bed. The vehicle roared off.

"David!" He reached the boy; his hand came down on David's shoulder. He tried to make out the license-plate number. But he could see only the last three numbers—six-eight-three.

"Are you all right?" he asked the boy, scanning for injuries. He saw none.

"I'm fine. Can you believe the nerve of those guys?" He slammed his fist into his palm. "What the hell were they trying to do?"

"I don't think you want to know. And you'd better not let your mother hear you cuss."

"The creeps tried to kidnap me, didn't they? Thanks for coming along, Luke."

"You're welcome." Luke grinned. This kid continually amazed him. "I saw that shin-kick that had one of them hopping. Good job." He gave the boy's shoulder a brief squeeze. "Come on. Let's get back to your mom."

Alexandra had already dismissed the area near the track as a target for their search. Much of the crowd had thinned and that area was almost deserted. She stepped up onto the bumper of a pickup. Her gaze scanned back and forth in the direction Luke had taken.

She spotted the red shirt immediately. She set off running, leaving Maggie staring after her.

When she reached her son, she clasped him to her breast, murmuring his name over and over. "Thank God, you're all right!"

David bore the display of affection stoically for a minute, then he tried to squirm free. "I'm fine, Mom." Then in a softer voice, "Mom, please." She released him reluctantly.

But when David stepped back, and saw what his mother's condition was, he threw himself into her arms again. "God, Mom, your knees are scraped. Your face—did they get you, too?" he cried.

She smoothed his hair back and forced herself to smile. "No, honey. They tried to scare me but they didn't really hurt me."

"Then why is your arm swollen?"

She saw that her forearm and elbow were indeed puffy, but she hadn't noticed. "I'm fine." She gave him another hug. "We're both fine. Thanks to Luke."

Luke shifted restively as she looked up at him, her gratitude—and something else—in her expression.

"How can I ever thank you?" she asked. For this brief second, her beautiful sea green eyes with their thick lashes spoke to him alone. The honeyed richness of her voice poured over, into and around *only* him, undermining his will to resist, sapping his strength. And making him feel like the most powerful man in the world. She was Circe.

Hell, why struggle?

"Oh, I'm sure Luke will think of a way," said David perceptively.

Both adults frowned at him but his smile didn't falter.

Morris and Maggie agreed to take care of getting Luke's car, the trailer and the racer back to the city, so that Luke could drive David and Alexandra.

She was deeply grateful; her hands had not yet stopped shaking.

Making sure Alexandra had fastened the dead-bolt lock behind her, Luke headed for his condo long enough to shower and change out of his racing gear. Then he rejoined them to wait for the FBI agent to arrive.

She had vetoed a trip to the emergency room to have her arm x-rayed. "It isn't broken. Just bruised. I'll put some ice on it."

David watched television. Alexandra wandered aimlessly round the room, holding her arm in a makeshift sling Luke had improvised to hold the ice bag to her elbow.

Restless, she needed something to fill this time. She offered Luke and David food, which they both declined. She stopped occasionally to touch David's hair or his hand.

David finally spoke. "Don't you think you'd feel better if you sat down, Mom?"

Alexandra sat on the edge of a chair. "I'm sorry you missed your party," she said to Luke.

He glared at her. "Don't be ridiculous."

She rose and began to pace again.

David decided that he could watch TV better in her bedroom.

"I'm making him nervous, aren't I?" she asked Luke. "Do I make you nervous, too?"

"Hell, yes, but not in the same way at all." Luke drew her down onto the sofa beside him. He held her hand, palm up, in his larger one. Her fingers were slightly curled. One by one he straightened them, leaving a warm, moist kiss at the base of each.

By the time he finished, Alexandra felt like a melting heap of candle wax, and the heat from his mouth had traveled up her arm and across her shoulders. She let her head fall back against the cushions and rolled her face toward him like a newly opened rose seeking the sustenance of the sun.

He was an exciting collection of contradictions. The planes of his face, the ones in shadow, were a dark contrast to the lighted side of his face. His mouth was beautiful, a strong, masculine combination of straight lines and curves. His jaw was square, trustworthy and a bit ruthless.

He was still studying the hand he held. His thick, black lashes hid his eyes from her; but, as she watched, mesmerized, he raised his gaze to hers. She caught her breath when she saw the fire, kindled in those silvery depths.

Her hand moved of its own accord to touch his cheek. The day's growth of whiskers rasped under her fingers. The sensation was not at all unpleasant; she smiled.

Luke felt the effect of Alexandra's beautiful smile all through his body. It sealed the breath in his throat, weakened his limbs, warmed the area around his heart and stoked the fire in his belly. "You're a delicate thing to pack such a powerful punch," he said.

"You said that to me once before."

"And I meant every word of it. You leave me reeling." His voice sounded like a truck with transmission problems. He cleared his throat. "Alex, I still want you. And somehow, we're going to be together. You can take that as a warning or a promise, either one."

She hesitated, her gaze dropping away from his.

"Don't say no. God, if you knew how much—"

She touched his mouth with the tips of her fingers. "I'm not saying no, Luke," she told him softly. "I'm just saying that I have to think about it for a while." She paused. "It won't be easy."

His heart leapt within his chest.

And the doorbell rang.

When David answered the door, Zarcone apologized for the delay. He laid his hat on the coffee table. "I stopped by to pick up a copy of the mug shot." He held it out to Luke. He also carried Alexandra's sketchbook. This he gave to her. "I promised I would return it."

"Yes, thank you."

"That's the man," Luke said. He had already given the story to Zarcone on the telephone. "No doubt about it." He handed the picture to David.

"Yes, sir. That's him. The creep. And he had a dark van just like we saw the other night when they broke in here."

Zarcone looked at Alexandra. She had bathed and dressed in a clean shirt and walking shorts, but the visible symbols of the attack were there on her legs, her face, her arm and, most dominantly, in her expression. "Can you identify him, too, Mrs. Prescott?"

"They put a blanket over my head. I didn't see either of the men."

"That's Ned Austin," Zarcone said.

Luke spoke up; his words were carefully chosen. "The van is a very dark navy blue with a thin gold stripe down each side. The same stripe outlines the tire wells. There is a chrome luggage rack on top and a spare-tire case on the back door, right-hand side. The last three numbers of the license are six-eight-three. Most of it was muddy, but I think it was a Georgia tag. The windows were smoked. I don't know much about vans but it looked to me like a pricey model."

By the time he finished, all three of them were gawking at him.

"I can't believe it," said David with an awed expression.

"Great job," said Zarcone finally. "May I use your phone?" he asked Alexandra.

"Surely. You'll have more privacy in the kitchen," she said, never taking her eyes off Luke.

"I was a lot closer to the van than you were and I didn't see all that," David said, now clearly put out with himself.

Luke reached over and ruffled the boy's hair. "You had other things to think about. Like drop-kicking some creep's shin."

"Oh, yeah." David grinned.

Chapter 7

Zarcone was back from the telephone in a few minutes. For the first time, the dapper man looked frazzled, an unusual sight. "The police are putting out an APB on the van immediately."

"Are they sending protection for Mrs. Prescott?" asked Luke.

Zarcone nodded. "A marked car will sit out front all night. They're assigning two men to her."

Luke nodded. "I'll be going, then."

"This is bad business, Quinlan. I don't mind telling you that I don't see much hope of getting the man behind the smuggling scheme. Ned Austin is just hired muscle. We may be able to get him on the attempted kidnapping charge and keep him in for a while. But he's been caught before. He's never broken. Just taken his prison time."

When Luke left Alexandra's, he noted with satisfaction that the police car was already on the street. He knocked on West's door.

West had been out when they returned from the track, but this time he answered. He was dressed in tuxedo pants and a shirt. "Hey, Luke. Come on in."

"I can't stay, West," Luke said grimly. "But I wanted to fill you in on what's happening." Luke watched the other man's face grow hard as he related the story of the afternoon. He could tell that West was truly shaken by the news. Some of the hardness eased when Luke explained about the police car.

"Attempted kidnapping is a serious charge."

"The men who locked Alexandra in the garage and tried to take David told her to stall the authorities for a week. They planned to keep David at least that long."

"If they *ever* planned to let him go. I didn't have any luck with the voice mail, but I decided to check out our illustrious client's address. I realized when I drove by that I happen to be very well-acquainted with a neighbor of Henderson's."

Luke could tell from his colleague's fiendish smile that this was news. "A girlfriend, I presume. Did you get anything from her?"

"She confirmed that the Hendersons are out of town. But when they get back, she's going to pry. She tells me she's exceptionally good at prying."

Luke chuckled. "Okay. And we'll call his office in the morning." He moved away. "I'll see you tomorrow, West."

"Hey, Luke?" West said as he was reaching for his key.

"Yeah?"

"Did you win?"

A pleased feeling skated through him and skimmed a smile across his face. "Yeah. Yeah, I did. Thanks for asking."

"Congratulations." He crossed his arms. "You know, there may be hope for you yet."

"What are you talking about?"

"The way you've loosened up lately. Less robotic. Since you began to pay attention to our neighbor, you've become almost human."

"Thank you," Luke said dryly. "You're not as obnoxious, yourself, when you're out of the office. Good night."

"Did you get a trophy to show off?"

Luke's face fell. "Hell, I forgot to pick it up."

"No!" Luke snapped. "Absolutely not!" He was suddenly, inexplicably outraged at the mere thought of Alexandra's being in danger again. His skin crawled; the hair on the back of his neck rose. He fought for control, unable to explain this dramatic response, even to himself.

"I beg your pardon?" Alexandra replied mildly.

"You're not going to make a target of yourself." He spun away from her and confronted the FBI agent. "What the hell are you thinking of, Zarcone?"

The agent had called him last night and asked him to meet at Alexandra's for coffee at 7:00 a.m. Now he said, "We'll still be watching her, naturally. The only difference is that we'll stay out of sight. It was her idea, Quinlan."

She began to pace, using the edge of an Oriental rug as a boundary. "Yes, it was my idea and it's my decision." A soft knit dress of buttercup yellow swirled around her knees as she turned, drawing Luke's gaze to her long shapely legs. "One week, that's what the men said," she said. "Maybe someone, maybe a murderer, will get away if something isn't done immediately."

"Let the police and the FBI handle it. That's what they get paid for."

"I want it over with. Our lives aren't our own anymore. I can't stand living like this. A policeman sitting on my doorstep. The calls—" She broke off the words, but it was too late.

"What calls?" both men demanded in unison. "Who?" Luke added.

Alexandra looked quickly at David, who was dressed and ready for school. She hated for him to hear this. But he didn't seem surprised. She wondered if he'd taken some calls himself.

"I don't know who. A voice I can barely hear whispers cusswords. The calls are probably not important."

"They bother you enough to mention them, and they're probably not important?" Zarcone pointed out the discrepancy in a mild tone.

She came to a chair and sat down hard. Some of the air seemed to go out of her. "You're right," she admitted. "After what happened yesterday, I can see that I should have told you."

Zarcone tactfully kept his mouth shut.

Luke returned to the original dispute. "Okay, so you want it over with. What about David? Are you willing to put the safety of your son on the line?" Luke demanded, gesturing toward the boy.

That was a low blow. She glared at him. "Of course I'm not. I'll make arrangements for David to visit a friend."

At that, David set his books aside and stood. "I want to stay here and help," David protested. "Mom, you need me."

"David, we'll talk about this later."

"No, Mom. Later will be *too* late." David's protest became as vehement as Luke's had been. He began to pace within the same boundaries that she'd used. "You aren't going to send me away."

"David, be careful what you say." Alexandra's voice held a warning note.

Luke could see the argument brewing and he took a long breath, wondering how best to diffuse the skirmish before it became a battle. Even with his own agitation, he could understand David's need to be involved. The boy's father was dead; his mother was all the family he had.

Luke had been down that road when he was not much older than David. As a male, albeit a juvenile one, the instinct to protect and defend was strong.

Alexandra's maternal urge to protect was equally strong. And she would not want an argument to cloud the issue for David.

"David, would you trust me to take care of your mother for you?" Luke asked the boy.

Alexandra frowned at his interruption. She opened her mouth, but Luke forestalled her protest with a gesture. "Would that ease your mind?" he asked, wanting to know.

"Ease his..." Alexandra shook her head in exasperation and faced Luke. She crossed her arms. "You are missing the point here. I'm his mother. I say he's going and that's final."

"Yes, if you give me your word," David said to Luke.

"You have it," Luke answered.

"Okay."

Luke turned to Alexandra, expecting to see impatience, even anger. What he did not expect to see was a complete shutting down of emotion. Her expression was blank, unreadable. He knew the reasons. He'd trampled on her territory without her consent. "I need to use your phone," he said abruptly.

"Certainly." She turned her back on him. He noted the stiff shoulders, the crossed arms.

He called West, caught him just as he was leaving for the office. He had started to disclose why he was going to be late this morning, when West interrupted. "I'm coming over," he said.

"David can stay with my folks," West said when the situation had been explained to him.

"We couldn't impose," Alexandra protested.

West persisted. "No one would ever think of looking for David at their house. Dad has a driver who can get David to school and back safely. Marvin's built like a Mack truck."

"I think it's a good idea." Zarcone spoke for the first time since the dispute had begun. "There is certainly no connection to tie Mr. Chadwick's parents to this case. It might be the safest place for the boy."

Alexandra looked from David to West to Luke. She didn't know what to do. But her first priority was David's safety. At last she sighed. "If you're sure they won't mind."

"I'm sure," West said. "I'll call them now and you can talk to them. They'll reassure you."

"We can use the phone in the kitchen." The two of them disappeared.

Zarcone turned to Luke. "It will take me several hours to get this set up. We'll leave the two men on duty outside for now."

Luke hesitated. "Are you sure you won't pull them off for a few hours?"

"I'm sure. I won't leave her unprotected, Quinlan. You have my word."

Luke didn't stop to ask himself why the agent deferred to him on the matter of Alexandra's safety. "I have some things to do at the office, pick up files to work on, turn others over to someone else. Do me a favor? Make certain I'm back before they leave?"

"I can do that," Zarcone said, nodding slowly. "So you'll be here with her, too."

"Yes," Luke said in a purposeful tone. "Chadwick has agreed to cover for me at the office. If I need to, I can use my vacation time."

The next few minutes passed with a flurry of activity. Alexandra and David went to his room to pack. West would drop him off at his parents' house and come back for Luke. They figured it would be more effective if they went to see Henderson together.

Besides, Luke remembered at the last minute that Maggie had his car.

"I'll be back as soon as I can," he told Alexandra. "Will you promise me that you'll stay inside?"

"Zarcone's men are around somewhere. You don't have to come back at all."

"I know that," he said sharply. "I want to. Okay?"

She didn't answer and he gave a heavy sigh. Without thinking what he was doing, he reached for her and pulled her into his arms. To his surprise, she didn't protest but relaxed against him, tucking her head under his chin. He inhaled the fresh, floral scent that rose from her hair and closed his eyes for a minute, enjoying the sensation.

All of a sudden, he remembered what she'd said at the track. *I have a teenage son. I know that wouldn't stop a lot of people but it stops me.*

The son was now safely out of the condo for the night. Maybe several nights. He felt guilty for the swoop of anticipation that quickened his heartbeat.

"Look, we'll get through this, Alexandra. But right now, both West and I, and David, would feel more comfortable if we take a few extra precautions."

The fight seemed to leave her. "All right," she said in a desultory voice.

When West rang the doorbell a few minutes later, she walked with Luke to the door to greet him. "Did you get David settled?" she asked.

"Yes. Marvin was taking him to school and he'll be there to pick him up."

"Thank you, West." Her smile was warm and she squeezed his hand. "I really do appreciate this."

West smiled. "No problem."

Luke watched them from under a dark frown. He planted his feet; he didn't plan to move until he had a last word with Alexandra.

West shrugged. "I'll wait for you in the car." He left.

Luke said gruffly, "Stay inside. I won't be later than noon."

"You already told me that once."

He looked into her eyes for a long minute. "This will be over soon." Then he cradled her face between his palms and gave her a gentle, hungry kiss. "Lock the door after me," he said and was gone.

Alexandra turned the key in the dead bolt and stood leaning against the door for a moment, trying to decide where her gumption had gone. Finally, she straightened. She had things to do today.

Since she wasn't going anywhere, she changed into jeans and headed to her studio to work.

"Did you get copies of the pictures?" Luke asked West when they were in the car.

"Yeah," West answered grimly. He took two folded sheets from his pocket and dropped them on the seat. "But I don't know what we're going to do with them."

Luke picked them up and studied them for a minute; then he slid them into his jacket pocket. "I don't want to link Alexandra to us, but maybe we'll think of something else to use them for."

"We could lose our jobs over this," West said.

"I don't give a damn if I do."

The statement brought West's head around. "What are you saying? As hard as you worked to get hired into this firm?"

"Yeah, I know. I can hardly believe it myself." Luke stared through the windshield into the middle distance. "The most prestigious firm in Atlanta, the most progressive city in the South. A lawyer would be a fool to walk away from the opportunity." He eased his back against the seat restlessly. "Well, I've been in the firm for almost ten years now." He sighed. "Practicing law that way isn't as fulfilling as I thought it would be."

To his surprise, West laughed.

Luke looked at him. "What's funny? Besides the obvious."

West touched a button. His window slid soundlessly into the door.

All at once the car was filled with September heat and the smell of fuel and exhaust from eight lanes of traffic. Over the noise of horns, a radio in the next car played the drive-to-work traffic report at top decibel. Rock and roll blasted from another, competing with the sounds of revving engines delivering a thousand other commuters into the city.

"When I graduated, this is the kind of law I thought I wanted to practice," West said with a strange smile. "Law down on the street, in the middle of things. Not the kind of law we practice at the firm—sanitary, sterile, insulated and protected from the masses in a high-rise ivory tower." He rolled the window up again.

"A friend from school wanted me to go in with him. A two-man firm."

"You? I don't believe it," Luke said flatly.

West shrugged. "Oh, my old man straightened me out pretty fast." He made a sound that might have been a sigh. "I guess he was right."

They were each lost in their own thoughts for a minute. Then West spoke again. "The guy is married now, has two kids, lives in the suburbs. I ran into him at a bar association meeting not long ago. He's not pulling down the bucks we are, but he's doing okay." A tinge of amazement colored his words. And Luke heard something else. Regret?

They had reached the exit that would take them to the offices of the man they sought, Paul Henderson. West peeled out of traffic onto a side street. He found a spot two blocks away from the building.

Luke was out of the car before it came to a stop. "Let's go."

"Hang on, Quinlan." West met Luke on the sidewalk and hurried to keep up with his long strides. "Don't go off half-cocked. Let's talk about this."

Luke did not slow his pace. "What's to talk about? We both saw the pictures. We both recognized Henderson. We want to know why he was dressed in a pilot's uniform." He smiled grimly. "It will be interesting to hear his excuse for that one."

"You know, Luke. We could be putting our necks on the line, too. We need to have a backup plan. If something happens to us, we won't be of much use to Alexandra."

"We'll tell him we've written everything down. If anything happens to us—et cetera. It's an outdated gimmick but it might work."

"Good idea," West observed wryly. "Even better if we'd done it."

"We will."

"I assure you that I have no idea what you are talking about," said Paul Henderson pleasantly. "I haven't been to the airport in weeks. And I certainly haven't gone there in a pilot's uniform. Who told you that they saw me?"

Luke and West had agreed that Alexandra's name could not be brought into it from their side. But their leverage was damned weak.

"You were seen, Mr. Henderson," said Luke evenly. "We wanted to give you an opportunity to explain why you were wearing someone else's clothes, before we answered to the authorities. They have questioned us in relation to another matter, which seems to tie in with the murder of a man who is suspected of smuggling computer technology." As a bluff it wasn't much but it was all he could come up with at the moment.

A flash of bright fury caught fire in Henderson's eyes. "You won't talk to the authorities at all, gentlemen. I am your client and, as such, rate confidentiality. If you take this ridiculous story to anyone, I will see that you are ruined. Not only will you be disbarred but I will sue you and the firm that employs you for an obscene amount of money. Would you be willing to wager on the outcome of such a suit?"

A heavy silence greeted his threat.

"I thought not. Now if you will excuse me, I have a full schedule this afternoon." Henderson pressed a button on his desk. When his secretary answered his summons, he informed her that his two visitors were leaving.

Luke led the way out, but just as he reached the threshold, he paused. "You will be available, won't you, Mr. Henderson?"

He had the satisfaction of seeing the older man's sudden frown before he elaborated, "In case we should need to discuss our other business further?"

Henderson's expression grew icy and brutal. "You know my business, Quinlan. I have no plans to leave town until you finish the papers I'm waiting for," he said.

When they were back in the car, West laughed. "Hot damn, we blindsided him. And he made a mistake, a big mistake. It works every time. If you can hand someone a big enough shock, they'll mess up."

"Excuse me? Did I miss something?" Luke said.

"He answered too quickly. He lied about not being in the airport at all that day. In a few minutes, he'll realize what he's done. He would have been better off if he'd said he was there for a perfectly innocent reason. What could we have argued?

"But he thinks he's too slick for us. So he lied."

Luke caught West's drift. He began to smile. The observation wiped away any lingering doubts that Henderson was somehow involved in this mess. They had been right to confront the bastard. "And his lie wasn't a nice safe lie, but one that can easily be disproven," Luke added.

"'Course, I don't know how much good it does. We still can't turn him in for questioning because he wears an unusual ring and dressed up in a pilot's uniform. And yet, all he had to do was sit tight."

Luke agreed. "Henderson's not very good at this. I'd say here is a man—a know-it-all kind of man but not a career criminal—who had an opportunity to make a lot of money fast. He can't stand the thought of *anyone* suspecting, so he tries a cover-up. Cover-ups rarely work. People who attempt them usually end up digging themselves in even deeper."

"He screwed up once. Maybe he'll screw up again," West said.

Luke answered slowly and thoughtfully. "Unless he's waiting for something besides the corporate papers. Why did the kidnapper tell Alexandra to stall the investigation for a week?" His voice took on an edge of excitement. "Say Henderson's tied into the death of the pilot. Say the man was killed because he tried to back out of an agreement, or didn't fulfill some part of a contract. Say the contract still hasn't been fulfilled."

"Henderson has a deadline!"

"Yeah. Someone may be threatening him," Luke said.

"A meeting, or something else so important that he can't leave town until it's done. So all we have to do is see that Alexandra and David are safe for a week. He'll be gone. They'll be okay. And we'll be off the hook."

Luke gave him a look of disgust. "You're willing to let this vermin get away with murder?"

"I don't see how we can prevent it without breaking confidentiality."

"Unfortunately, you're right. Let me off at the next corner," Luke said after a minute. He was depressed as hell. "I'll get a cab to my car."

Alexandra used the back of her hand to brush a strand of hair from her forehead. On the drawing board in front of her was her latest effort for a student science club at an Atlanta university.

Georgia Tech's mascot was a yellow jacket and the club wanted a variation for their annual party. She had come up with an appealing little fellow, a cross between a germ and a bug she called Mike Roy Biotic.

She wiped her hands before taping a piece of clear film to a strong piece of poster board. Then she slid her matted drawing underneath and secured it. She was searching for the right sized envelope when she heard the doorbell.

Startled, she dropped a handful of packing material and it slithered across the floor. "Drat."

The bell rang again. "Okay, I'm coming."

"Hi," said Luke with a melancholy expression that hadn't been there when he'd left earlier. He tried to smile.

Alexandra had always been quick to respond with sympathy and he seemed to need some. But, looking at him and remembering how tenderly he had held and comforted her this morning, she was suddenly hesitant.

"Hi, come on in. Make yourself at home. Excuse me, I was getting something ready for the mail." She didn't wait for him to answer but returned to her studio.

Luke took off his coat and loosened his tie. He wandered around the living room, checking out the titles on her bookshelves, her CDs. The glass doors opening onto the patio and the park area beyond were draped in sheer curtains to cut the glare. He moved aside the drapery and stood for a minute or two looking out. Now that school was in session, the park area was nearly deserted.

A couple of matrons batted a tennis ball back and forth, but their hearts didn't seem to be in the game. One of the grounds keepers raked around a flower bed.

He let the drapery fall and plunged his hands into his pockets. He jingled his change. He could hear Alexandra moving around somewhere in the background but the condo was too quiet.

Hell, he was not accustomed to doing nothing. And he was fully aware of his own heightened tension due to the fact that they were alone.

Not that he expected Alexandra to fall into his arms or anything, he told himself. Then he grinned. But a man could hope.

He looked at the television set and looked away. Watching Oprah or Geraldo wasn't his idea of filling time. Then he wandered down the hall in the direction of the sounds.

Alexandra's studio faced the same view he'd observed minutes ago. Sunlight poured in through these undraped windows. The room was neat and sparingly furnished. A colored illustration stood propped against her drawing board.

His urge was to approach, to have a look, but instead he stood silently at the door and watched her rummage through a closet, a slight smile lingering on his face.

She was on her knees, her shapely bottom in the air. Today she wore jeans and sneakers and a soft pink T-shirt that clung lovingly to her breasts and upper arms. Her hair was off her neck in a ponytail.

She backed out of the closet and sat on her heels. With a sigh, she hooked her hands on her hips.

"Something wrong?" he asked.

She spun so quickly that the ponytail slapped her cheek. "Don't *do* that! Don't sneak up on me." She returned to her search.

"Sorry." She didn't invite him in, but she didn't tell him to get out, either.

He entered the room and moved slowly along the walls, looking at her drawings. A few were framed and familiar, like the colorful prints of Christmas twins, Mary Lee and Holly Day. He'd seen them in an upscale mall boutique during the season. And the drawing of the librarian, Reid Moore, whose steel-rimmed glasses and quirky grin had proclaimed Library Week throughout the city last year. "I've said it before. You're really talented."

"Thanks."

Other characters caught his eye: Major Bucks—a Big-Daddy type with a large paunch, dressed in a white suit; a streetwise, macho male with abundant whiskers was named Al E. Katz; a wiry, youthful figure, bearing an amazing resemblance to David, darted from place to place within the margins of the page. She called that one Rick O'Shea. They were all funny, they were all appealing and the work was meticulous.

He was reminded again of the impetuous imagination, the sense of the ridiculous, the absurd—whatever—that would be essential for the creation of such work. And David telling him how much his mother had changed since his dad died. He found himself envying Daniel Prescott for having known her before all that intelligent humor was diluted by worry and responsibility.

He wandered last to the drawing board. His smile became a grin, then a chuckle. "Mike Roy Biotic? That's good. Who's it for? Someone at Georgia Tech obviously, since he's wearing the yellow jacket."

She sat on her heels again. "A science club. Do you really like it?"

"It's cute. But where are the politicians? I know you've done some."

Her smile was wry. "I keep them out of sight in a drawer."

She thought for a minute, then slapped her knees and stood up. "I have another drawing in that drawer. I did it to give you. But then—" she slid her gaze to him "—I wasn't sure how you felt about my sketches after the lecture you gave me on satire."

Luke grew very still. "You did a drawing for me?"

She went to a filing cabinet; the drawer in question rolled out on silent casters. She tilted her head to the side to read as she leafed through the folders. "Yes, not long after we met.'' She came up with what she was searching for and pushed the drawer closed with the thrust of her shapely hip. ''Here it is.''

Like the sketch on the drawing board, this one had been mounted under a clear protective coating. Luke took it, almost hesitantly, she thought. ''If you don't like it, you can just throw it away. I did it for fun and before I knew you very well.''

Luke hadn't taken his eyes off her, but now he looked at the sketch in his hands. The black-and-white illustration showed a very tall, very straight man in a suit and tie.

She had caught his features exactly with a minimum of exaggeration. His hair was neat, precisely parted; the glasses, the old horn-rims that he used to wear; the shoes, wing-tipped and shiny. His hands were by his side; one held a bulging briefcase. Papers trailed out of it and behind him in a path that stretched to the margin.

The surprise was the figure of blindfolded Justice, holding her scales, straddling his shoulders like a Fort Lauderdale beach bunny on spring break.

She had labeled the drawing ''Justin Case'' and had scrawled her signature across one corner.

Alexandra watched Luke examine her sketch with some apprehension. His pensive expression didn't give her a clue of what he was thinking. The drawing was innocuous, wasn't it?

Or was it too impertinent? Disrespectful? She rubbed her hands down the legs of her jeans.

He glanced up, a smile beginning to tilt one side of his mouth. She felt better. Then he looked back down and the smile faded.

Finally, she could stand it no longer. "You hate it," she declared. "Let me...I'll get rid of it." She held out her hand. "I'll do you another one some time."

He moved the drawing back, away from her wiggly fingers. "No. I do like it, very much. You say you're giving it to me?"

"Of course, if you want it." Her eyes narrowed. "And if you are going to offer to pay me, forget it."

He looked up, met her eyes. "I do want it. Thank you, Alexandra."

"You're welcome." She looked around her studio. "Now I *have* to find an envelope the right size for Mike Roy there."

She returned to the closet and Luke went back to the living room with his sketch. His heart was actually pounding like a kid's at Christmas. This was the first present he'd ever received that wasn't given for a holiday or birthday. A spontaneous gift like this—it threw him for a loop.

He needed to put some distance between them.

It was one thing to want a woman, want her so badly his teeth ached. It was quite another thing to be beholden, disarmed by an act of feminine kindness. Since he was sixteen years old—no, hell, long before that—he'd been on his own and he depended on no one but himself.

As a boy, his only functional weapons had been a healthy body and a good mind, and he'd used them to get where he was today. The navy had taught him the value of both training and conditioning; college and law school had sharpened his skills.

Nothing in his life, however, had prepared him to deal efficiently with softer feelings. So he made it a rule to avoid them.

Oh, he had soft feelings. He wasn't a cold-blooded monster. He felt tenderness; he could be gentle, soft-hearted, sympathetic. But early on, he'd seen the danger of being susceptible to those emotions. He'd refused to allow himself the luxury of caring too much.

Distance, that was what he needed, distance. And how the hell was he supposed to find that, given the circumstances?

He supposed he could let West take over guard duty. That alternative was so revolting that he rejected it immediately. He didn't have to ask himself why.

Alexandra came in a few minutes later to find him still staring at her drawing. She waved the wrapped and taped package. "I need to get Mikey in the mail. Any suggestions?"

Before he could answer, the telephone rang.

"Oh, God, no." Alexandra looked at him in alarm.

Chapter 8

"Hello," Alexandra answered tentatively. Instantly she relaxed and gave Luke a rueful smile. "It's West. He wants to speak to you."

Luke was still holding her drawing. He propped it against the bookshelf and took the telephone. "West? What's up?"

"We have been summoned to appear in Bolton's inner sanctum after lunch."

Luke had been expecting the summons, but not straightaway. He was surprised Henderson had not given himself more time to think. But then look at the knee-jerk reaction he'd had to their visit. West had been right when he'd observed that Henderson had screwed up once, now twice. Maybe he would screw up again.

Suddenly, he was distracted by a glance at Alexandra. The alarm had faded from her eyes, but she was grasping her elbows in an unconsciously self-protective gesture. The sight of her anxiety made his blood boil. No woman, no *one*, should be frightened every time the telephone rang. "Ah, hell," he said hotly.

West misunderstood his response. "I endorse that sentiment completely. Henderson didn't waste any time. How soon can you get here?"

"Hang on a minute." He put down the phone and went to check the peephole in the front door. As he passed, he gave Alexandra's arm a reassuring squeeze.

The police car was still parked outside. He came back to tell West, "I'll be there as soon as the traffic will allow."

He hung up, grabbed his coat and shrugged into it. "I have to go to the office. I'll be back as soon as I can," he told her as he tightened the knot of his tie. "The police are still parked outside." He smoothed his collar. "Zarcone promised he would make sure I was here before they left. Don't forget—"

"'Lock the door and don't go outside.'" She repeated his words from this morning. "I'm not going to do anything stupid, Luke."

That was better, thought Luke. He'd rather see her feisty than afraid, any day. He grinned, took the package she was holding and dropped a tender kiss on her lips. "Thanks for the drawing. I'll send Mike Roy on his way for you. Regular or express mail?"

The taste of the brief kiss lingered long after he left the complex, long after he drove from the side streets onto the interstate, which would take him downtown. When he was halfway to the office, he remembered his vow to put distance between them.

* * *

Luke arrived at the tall building in the heart of
downtown and took the elevator to the twenty-seventh
floor, the top of four floors occupied by the firm, and
the floor on which the senior partners' offices were
located. Where the other three floors were usually active, bustling and, on occasion, frenetic, the twenty-
seventh was dignified, tranquil and eternally hushed.
The telephones bells were muffled, the secretaries
murmured instead of talked and no one's pace was
more than sedate, no matter who the client happened
to be.

Bolton's secretary informed Luke that he was forty-
seven minutes early. A hanging offense, she implied
with haughty-but-proper look.

"I'll be in my office," Luke said, not at all intimidated. The delay would give him time to get files together to work on at home.

Forty-five minutes later, West appeared in the
doorway to Luke's office. "Ready for the firing
squad?" he asked.

"Almost," said Luke. He indicated the files on his
desk. "These are the cases you may get calls about.
I'm taking these others back to the condo. I should be
able to get some work done there."

"If you can accomplish that, you are a better man
than I," West said with a grin.

Luke scowled but didn't take the bait.

"I don't give a good damn if the client turns out to
be a murderer, a lawyer doesn't threaten to betray
confidentiality!"

Instead of offering them a chair, Bolton had kept them standing side by side in front of his desk like errant schoolboys. At the word *murderer* Luke felt West shift uneasily.

The senior partner was wound up. His face was alarmingly red and a vein in his temple throbbed visibly. His heated diatribe had been going on for nearly ten minutes.

For a flash, Luke was tempted to tell the pompous old windbag where he could shove this job, but he was afraid the shock would precipitate a stroke. That he could entertain such a notion astonished him. What *would* it do to a man with high blood pressure?

Bolton continued, "If Mr. Henderson wants to move his business to the moon, you will do the paperwork, do you understand? And you will not presume to tell him when he can or cannot leave town. And you certainly will not tell anyone else what his plans are."

West opened his mouth. "Sir, that wasn't—"

"Quiet! Besides being a close friend of mine, Henderson's annual fees to this firm are more than enough to hire four lawyers to take your places. I hope that is clear enough for you."

"Yes, sir," said West stonily. "Except for formal appointments, we will make every effort to stay out of Mr. Henderson's way."

"No, you won't do that, either, Mr. Chadwick," Bolton said sarcastically. "Henderson will be an honored guest at my retirement dinner, sitting at my own table. You are to fall all over yourselves, lick the damned floor in front of his feet if you have to, but alleviate any ill feelings this man has toward you. Do you understand?''

Luke's emotions were as tight as an overblown balloon, ready to explode at any moment. Every muscle, every nerve was stretched to the limit. That was it. All he could take. The image of himself, on his knees in front of a bastard like Henderson, who would menace women and children and do God-knows-what-else, threatened his sanity, not to mention his self-respect. He opened his mouth, fully intending to resign on the spot.

But Bolton suddenly turned on the charm for which he was famous. "Boys, boys," he said expansively. "You know how this business works. We may not like or even approve of some of our clients, but under the Constitution, even the most heinous criminals are guaranteed representation. I am assuming that your loyalty to the firm, which has launched both of you into vastly superior positions to the majority of your classmates, is absolute. When you've been around as long as I have . . ."

At that, Luke tuned him out. He agreed with the philosophy of the Constitution, but he had always had a certain difficulty representing people he didn't value or respect.

However, Bolton had inadvertently introduced another subject that deserved some further thought. Loyalty.

His loyalty to the firm *had* been absolute. He'd designated his goals when he was sixteen years old. His name on the letterhead of this company had helped him reach those goals. He enjoyed the advantages, the prestige, the prosperity.

But he had given the members of the firm their money's worth, too. He'd brought with him a good mind and a willingness to work. Sixteen, eighteen hours a day for nearly ten years—a large chunk out of his life.

Yes, they'd definitely gotten their money's worth. He mustn't lose sight of that fact.

Luke arrived, loaded down with files and books. He was much later than he'd planned to be, but Zarcone was true to his word; the car had remained until he got home.

Alexandra let him in. She was still dressed in the jeans and pink T-shirt. She seemed relieved to see him. Or was she just restless at being confined? "You can work in the dining room if you like," she offered.

He disposed of his burden carefully on her shining dining room table and straightened. "Thanks, this will be fine. You're sure I won't be in your way?"

"David and I usually eat in the kitchen. The table in there is large enough for two."

"Something smells terrific," he said.

And feels damned peculiar, he added to himself. A stiffness had risen between them that had not been there when he'd kissed her goodbye. He dipped his chin and studied her face. "You had another call," he guessed. He knew from her expression that his hunch was right.

"Yes, I did. This time the caller didn't whisper. He spoke right up."

"The devil he did! What did he say?"

"Same thing he said at the Road Atlanta. That I should keep my mouth shut when the police come around if I wanted to keep my son safe." Her tone was bitter but her eyes, when she looked up at him, were vulnerable again.

"Alexandra, they don't know where David is. And there's no way for them to find out," he said firmly, forcefully. "Please don't torture yourself." He grasped her arm, intending to bring her closer, but she resisted, her hand flat on his chest.

"There's more. He says that I shouldn't count on my friends, the two lawyers, for protection."

Shock sent chills through him. "What?" he barked sharply.

That Henderson, or his proxy, would do something so shameless and blatant spooked the hell out of him. Nobody else knew he and West were involved. The man was deliberately taunting them.

He combed his hand through his hair in a gesture of frustration. Had he and West increased the danger to Alexandra and David? His first thought was to get in touch with West right away. Then Zarcone.

"I called Zarcone."

With the words, her resistance seemed to fade, while his increased. Nevertheless, as if with a will of its own, his hand closed around her shoulder and he pulled her close. She felt so good relaxing against him; she fitted precisely into that spot under his arm.

Would Zarcone suspect that he and West were holding out on him? He squeezed her upper arm absently. "I'm glad you called him right away. What did he say?"

She lowered her thick, sun-tipped lashes for a moment, then raised them and tilted her head back to rest on his shoulder. "He said that he'd look into it," she said softly.

Her skin took on a flushed rosiness that looked like a warm ripe peach. Her fragrance, a mixture of a floral bouquet with something spicy thrown in, went straight to his head.

Luke was torn in two directions, so much so he thought he'd lose his mind.

In one direction was Alexandra, warm and receptive and sexy as hell and heaven combined, standing hip to hip with him. If he handled this right, they could become a great deal closer before the night was over. The brush of their clothing was like a provocative whisper. The heat from her soft hand on his chest tantalized him. He had to battle the urge to cover her hand with his, to guide it downward until her fingers warmed his sex. There might never be another chance as promising as this one.

He closed his eyes, then opened them again, feeling something akin to pain. On the other hand, he had to stay focused on the danger that faced her and David. "What does Zarcone mean by 'looking into it'?"

She sighed. "I don't know. Right now, I don't even care. I'm so tired, I can hardly think straight. Why don't we have an early supper? I've been cooking this afternoon—comfort food."

Luke's own mind was trying to function with frustrating speed, switching back and forth between two propositions, like a spectator at a tennis match who's never quite sure where the ball is.

But he was distracted by her description. "Comfort food?"

"Comfort food, soul food, whatever. Corn bread, turnip greens, black-eyed peas, country ham. Maybe it will take my mind off the call."

Luke scratched his ear. Was it his imagination or was her soft drawl drawn out even more? He knew the pitch was lower because shivers had traveled up his spine as she named the dishes. He'd never eaten turnip greens or black-eyed peas, and country ham was too salty for his taste. But if she wanted comfort food—her fingers had worked their way under his tie and between the buttons of his shirt. She had no idea what she was doing to him.

Did she?

He shook his head to clear it.

Fool that he was to relinquish this opportunity, he had to get hold of West. They needed to hash out this situation and come up with a workable plan. They were dealing with a cunning man. They had to be more cunning, more creative and clever, more resourceful.

It took an overabundance of arrogance for Henderson to reveal himself by calling Alexandra.

Or *was* it Henderson?

He turned her face so he could look into her eyes. It was almost his downfall, but he watched for a reaction as he asked, "Sweetheart, did you recognize the voice?"

Luke didn't seem to notice the endearment, but Alexandra did. She noticed and she cherished the idea that it had come out so... impulsively. "Zarcone said that, from my description—the voice was weird—it could have been computer-modified."

"We're going to put a recorder on your phone," Luke said decisively.

Suddenly, her pleasant mood was gone. Luke was absorbed by the phone calls and Zarcone and everything but her. She did not blame him; she should have been fixed on the danger, too. But his informal presence in her home raised her level of awareness more than she had expected. She had a difficult time keeping her eyes off this easygoing, laid-back Luke.

"It's already been done," she told him, suddenly weary of it all. "One more blow to freedom, liberty and independence."

"Don't." He laid his hand atop her head. "You'll get your freedom back, Alexandra. Don't think of this as a permanent affliction. I'll be out of your way before you know it."

"Yes, I recognize that." She gave him a bland smile before she extricated herself from his arms and headed for the kitchen.

After dinner he helped her with the dishes. "I like comfort food," he said. He dried and held up her iron skillet, which, she had informed him, could never be put in the dishwasher. "Where does this go?"

"Under the cabinet beside the stove," she instructed. "I'm glad you enjoyed it." She wiped the counter, folded the towel and put it away. "Coffee?"

"Yes, please."

She poured them each a cup.

"I hope you don't mind," he said when they had moved, with their coffee, into the living room. She sat curled in a corner of the sofa, facing him. "I've asked West to come over here. We have to work some on contracts." He avoided looking at her when he gave the false excuse. He hated lying to her but he couldn't tell her the truth, dammit.

He had called West earlier while she was finishing the preparations for the comfort food. He smiled at the name. West agreed they had to talk.

"No, I don't mind at all." But she *was* disappointed, Alexandra admitted to herself. She had looked forward to sitting down after dinner, talking, getting to know this man who was occupying more and more of her thoughts. More than was wise. She leaned forward to set her cup on the coffee table and rose to her feet.

"Don't go." Luke snagged her hand; he tugged her closer. To her surprise, she let herself be tugged. She knelt with one knee on the sofa cushion, the other foot on the floor.

Luke curled his hands around her waist and looked at her. At his eye level, soft pink cotton molded her upper body, her sleek midriff and—oh, God—her high, firm breasts. "You're so pretty, so pretty," he murmured unsteadily.

She held herself still, did not protest as he slid his hands up her sides. He bracketed her breasts and gently lifted as he squeezed them together forming a strip of tantalizing cleavage above the scoop neckline of her shirt. As he watched, her nipples hardened.

She laid her hands on his shoulders to steady herself. Her breathing became rapid. "Don't . . . look at me like that, like you can see through my clothes," she whispered hoarsely. "I can't bear it, Luke."

He looked up then, into her green eyes, afraid that he had done something to disgust her. But her pupils were dilated slightly, her mouth was moist where she'd bitten her lips and her eyelids had lowered under the weight of desire.

She was as hot as he was.

He felt a primitive surge of emotion flood through him, leaving him hard and desperate. He wanted to lay her down on the sofa right now. He wanted to strip off her shirt, her jeans. He wanted to explore, to caress, to kiss, every inch of her beautiful body. He wanted— oh, how he wanted to bury himself deep inside her.

How had this gotten so out of hand at such a breakneck speed? One minute he'd grabbed her hand, intending to say, "Stay, don't leave. Stay and talk."

And the next minute, passion had flamed to demanding life.

He reached up to slide his fingers around the back of her neck. He pulled her down until their lips were millimeters apart. The skin at her nape was warm and smooth. He moved his thumb and felt her shiver. "Kiss me," he demanded.

She caught her breath at his challenge. Then she parted her lips and closed the space between them.

When he felt the touch of her lips, Luke kept a tight rein on his reaction. He knew instinctively that he was the first man in four years. He didn't want to scare her away; he wanted her to feel comfortable with him. But after a taste of her innate sensuality, he found that keeping a leash on the erotic craving that ate through him was damn near impossible.

Her tongue was sweet, so sweet, as she probed his mouth. When she slid her fingers into his hair and sucked his lower lip, he groaned, his heart pounding like a runaway train, and crushed her to him. His own tongue joined hers in the undulating dance of passion. His hands moved restlessly, hungrily, all over her back, across her shoulders, down to cup her rounded bottom.

The doorbell rang. Luke let loose a string of curses that would have blistered the ears of a sailor.

Alexandra rested her forehead on his. "Your bright idea. Not mine," she said huskily. They got to their feet, neither of them at all steady. No longer was she the tallest, no longer the one in charge. He continued to move his hands on her—now they stroked her upper arms. She felt sad, bereft.

He read her like a book. His mouth twisted ruefully. "Alexandra, it's important. I wouldn't have called him otherwise."

"I understand, Luke. Really I do."

When West arrived he was distracted, affected by the same sort of mood as Luke. He poured himself coffee when she offered it, then he and Luke disappeared into the dining room.

She didn't know whether to be offended or not when they closed the door firmly between the two rooms. It wasn't as though she would deliberately listen to their business, or that she would understand it if she did. She finished her coffee, took the cup to the kitchen and rinsed it.

Rather than stay in the living room where the drone of their voices was audible but not the words, she went to her room. Before she got ready for bed, she called David. He seemed to be happy enough.

She bathed, and brushed her teeth. Finally, she climbed into bed and pulled the sheet up over her. She lay there for a long time, staring at the ceiling and thinking.

This evening had certainly turned out differently from what she'd expected. And thought she wanted, at the time. Now that she could look back on those moments, though, she realized that she should be scared witless.

Never had she responded like that to a man. Never.

It seemed that all he had to do was kiss her and she completely lost sight of who and where she was. She was too aroused, too provocative, too passionate when she was with him.

Early the next morning, Luke stood with his hands in his pockets at the window overlooking the quadrangle behind Alexandra's condo.

He had spent the night here, in David's very interesting room, but he'd risen before daylight, cadged Alexandra's keys from her dressing table—and resisted with a giant will the temptation to crawl into her bed.

He left briefly, returning to his place to shower and dress. He couldn't bring himself to move clothes into her home.

He put on jeans and his running shoes. Not that he had any plans to run. But the shoes gave him an idea.

Last night had not turned out as he'd expected. He and West had talked until well after midnight and resolved nothing. The problem was, deadline or not, Henderson was being very cagey. Maybe if the police caught Austin and he could be convinced to talk—

He heard soft noises from the kitchen. In a few minutes, the smell of frying bacon reached his nostrils and he realized he was hungry. He walked to the kitchen door. Alexandra was still in her robe, a floor-length, zipped-to-the-throat affair. He smiled to himself, wondering what she was wearing under it.

Her back was characteristically straight. She moved with grace as she flipped bacon onto a waiting paper towel, though he knew she had to be anxious.

"Can I help?" he asked, startling her. "Sorry."

"Yes, you can set the table," she said stiffly when she regained her breath. "Place mats and napkins are in the top drawer of the buffet." She reached for the eggs and began cracking them into a bowl.

He nodded and withdrew. She was oddly subdued this morning. He could understand that, he was feeling the same way. To be so aroused, so hot, and have to turn it off like a spigot—last night was a lost opportunity that he might regret more as time passed.

He took green, woven mats and napkins from a drawer and brought them to the kitchen table, lining them up carefully parallel to the edge. "Silverware?" he asked.

"In the buffet, second drawer," she answered without turning.

The task was completed too quickly. Once again he stood beside the table watching her move efficiently through her kitchen. "Anything else?"

Alexandra glanced up. Luke stood with one shoulder against the wall, hands thrust into the pockets of his well-worn jeans. He had on a fresh blue shirt, open at the throat, with the sleeves folded back to his elbows.

No man had the right to look that exciting in the morning. She was fully aware of how she herself looked, with her carelessly combed hair and sexless robe. She should have dressed before she came into the kitchen, but this was the way her morning routine went, and she hadn't thought about changing it until it was too late.

She concentrated on scrambling the eggs. "This is nearly ready. You can pour the juice and coffee. Jelly is in the refrigerator, if you like it."

Silently, they finished the preparations and finally it was time to sit down. Together. Luke held her chair.

Alexandra offered him the platter of bacon and eggs. He passed her the basket filled with buttered toast. She took a piece, bit into the crisp bread and flinched. The crunch of her chewing seemed to echo in the hush between them. She met his eyes, saw amusement there and looked away.

At last the interminable meal was over. Luke rose, taking his plate and glass to the sink. Alexandra followed. "More coffee?" she asked.

"No, thanks."

"Excuse me, then. I'll get dressed."

Luke spread his papers out on the dining room table and tried to concentrate. The sound of water rushing through the pipes, however, was a major distraction. All he could see when he stared down at the legalese was Alexandra, naked in the shower—or bath. He wondered which.

He could easily picture her standing under the spray, water running from her wet hair, off her breasts, over her belly, down her long, beautiful legs. But he could just as easily picture her reclining beneath a layer of bubbles, her hair curly and pinned haphazardly on top of her head, lifting one leg to squeeze a spongeful of lather on her calf, her thigh.

He groaned and shifted in his chair, easing the pressure of his jeans.

Alexandra came out of her room, determination in her stride. Luke was in the living room, staring out the window. She was surprised not to find him working but that fit right into her plans. "Listen, Luke."

He dropped the side of the sheer drape and turned. She swallowed against a sudden dryness in her throat. He was so good-looking. "I can't stand this quiet. I want to do something," she stated, ready to argue.

"I was thinking about that earlier. Would you like to go to my health club for a workout?"

Well, that had been easy enough, thought Alexandra fifteen minutes later. They were on their way into the city. She didn't know what arrangements had been made, but Luke had been on the phone with Zarcone for ten of those fifteen minutes. The FBI man seemed to think a trip downtown was a good idea.

Knowing she was bait was hard for Alexandra. But being alone in the condo with Luke was the real hazard.

"Have you talked to David?" Luke asked after they had returned to the car. They'd spent all morning at the health club. Alexandra had jogged and sweat, joined an aerobics class and sweat some more. Now she felt like a different person, more relaxed, stronger.

The tension that she'd been living with had knotted her muscles more than she realized. So she'd finished with a pummeling massage, and her shower had dissipated the last traces of achiness.

She'd dressed again in the khaki skirt and white safari shirt she'd hurriedly donned when Luke had issued his invitation. She hadn't taken time to dry her hair, just pulled it back from her face and twisted it into a bundle at her nape. She had no makeup with her. She hadn't thought it mattered, but now she wished she'd made just a bit more effort to look nice.

"Yes, last night. He's fine." She studied him from across the seat. He drove, as he did everything, with confidence and mastery. His dark brown hair was damp from the shower and his face was slightly flushed from exertion.

"Thank you for suggesting the health club, Luke. It helped a lot."

"Would you like to go somewhere for lunch?" He glanced in the rearview mirror. "I notice that we still have Zarcone's man with us."

"I can't," she said, dismayed to realize that she wanted to go into a restaurant on the arm of this man, but when she did, she wanted to be dressed in her very finest. "Look at my hair—my clothes are a mess and I haven't a smidgen of makeup on."

Luke took his eyes off the road for the briefest glimpse of her. "You look beautiful," he said in a low, husky voice.

She didn't doubt for a minute that he was trying to make her feel better, but the compliment warmed her face, made her heart flutter and her lips yearn for the taste of his. "Thank you. That was a good try."

He opened his mouth to tell her that every word was the truth, so help him, God. Instead, he grinned. "We'll go someplace casual. How about the zoo? They have great hot dogs."

Chapter 9

Alexandra fell asleep on the way back to the complex. Now and then, Luke glanced at her, curled on the seat beside him. Her hair, which had been wet and slick, had dried free to curl around her face, softening her features.

As he drove, it began to rain, an easy, soaking rain. The streetlights alternated with the darkness, tagging her face with silver highlights, then retreating.

She was an extraordinary woman. Smart and beautiful, a good mother, a talented artist. This day, spent together in the most commonplace activities, had reinforced his opinion that she was a welcome and witty friend, besides being sexy as hell.

Their dramatic responses to each other, triggered last night by their brief encounter before West arrived, had engulfed them both with a startling swiftness—even more than the day at the track.

He wanted her and he was sure she wanted him. So why was he still wary about making love to her? Why did he still feel the itch to put distance between them?

If she had been feeling as unsteady as he was this morning, then getting through the day had promised to be touchy. So he'd called Zarcone and set up today's activities.

Zarcone had been reluctant, but Luke had reminded him, with an intensity that was uncharacteristic, of Alexandra's cooperation with the authorities from the very first. "She deserves this, Zarcone. Her life has been disrupted, her safety and that of her son has been threatened. She needs to get away from everything that will remind her for a few hours."

"Okay, okay," Zarcone had grumbled.

She shifted in her sleep, began to stir.

Hell, he could have her and distance, too.

Just because they made love, they didn't necessarily have to make promises.

He pulled into his parking space and turned off the engine. The soft drumming of raindrops on the roof of the sedan and the ting of the cooling engine were the only sounds.

Alexandra awakened slowly, unaware of her surroundings, but without feeling any anxiety or apprehension. She knew that Luke was nearby somewhere.

She moved her shoulders, stretched her arms in front of her, turning her linked fingers inside out. She yawned—discreetly. Finally, she opened her eyes.

And smiled, that pretty curve of her lips, which activated a dimple. "Hi," she said.

Luke was as weak as a day-old kitten by the time she spoke. He swallowed hard. "Hi, yourself. We're home."

Home. What a lovely sound the word had, thought Alexandra, like a comforting mantra. She sat up and looked around. "And it's raining," she said in surprise as she unbuckled her seat belt. "How long have you been driving in the rain?"

"Ever since we hit the perimeter. It wasn't a bad drive, though—the traffic was light." He opened his door and got out.

The dome light came on and Alexandra cringed, knowing what she must look like. He reached into the back seat for the bag containing her exercise gear.

When she hesitated before getting out, he stuck his head back inside. "Do you need an umbrella?"

"Goodness, no." She got out of the car and scooted up the pathway to the porch. Nevertheless, they were both wet by the time they got inside. He followed her into the kitchen.

"How about coffee?" she asked. "It won't take a minute to fix."

"Sounds good."

She took the bag from him and put it in the tiny laundry cubicle off the kitchen. She used a towel there to dry her face and arms, then tossed it to him.

"Do something for me," Luke asked when they were seated at the kitchen table over steaming mugs of coffee.

She propped her chin on her hand. Her green eyes glimmered with amusement. "Should I be wary?"

"Let you hair all the way down. I've only seen it that way a couple of times."

"I always wear it up in the summer. It's too hot on my neck." Alexandra laughed self-consciously as she reached back to release the barrette that held the twisted bundle. "It's already fallen almost all the way down—ouch, I'm caught."

"Here, let me." Luke was on his feet and around the table. His fingers made quick work of the disorder, while setting off a few shimmers of excitement on her scalp. Then they remained to finger-comb through the strands. She thought he leaned down to inhale the scent, but she wasn't sure.

"Your hair is beautiful—the colors are like sunshine and moonlight." His voice was low and slow and infinitely seductive.

A smile curved her lips. Luke Quinlan, romantic? It was a lovely thing to say. "Thank you."

When he returned to his seat, she was stunned to see the flames that ignited in his pewter eyes.

They had spent the day in easy camaraderie, first at the health club, then the zoo. Later, they had driven out to Stone Mountain Park, east of the city. They had ridden the paddleboats and wandered through the park itself. No suggestive glances, no molten touches, had inhibited the day.

Though he had held her hand for a while, he had kept things light between them. Light and diverting and fun. Deliberately, she thought. She had just about convinced herself that she liked it this way. At least for now. At least until the ordeal was over.

But now, looking into those hot gray eyes and becoming ensnared like a rabbit in a hunter's headlights, she knew she had been fooling herself. She could not have looked away if her life had depended upon it.

Her heartbeat became audible in her ears.

The silence in the room was heavy with demands and promises. Her body responded instantaneously to both. The blood rushed through her to nourish all the secret places, readying them for a glorious experience. She felt the dampness between her thighs; her nipples were suddenly sensitive, as though abraded by the touch of a callused thumb. Taking a breath, one efficient enough to sustain her, became an effort.

He reached for her hand and held it between his palms, disturbing but not breaking the spell. "Your skin is so smooth, so soft." He looked down at their joined hands, and she followed his gaze. Her hand was totally swallowed by his.

She licked her dry lips. "Luke, I haven't been with a man since—"

His self-satisfied grin cut off her words as surely as if he'd muffled her mouth with his hand. She realized that she had been assuming a lot, when he hadn't actually said a word.

No, that wasn't true. He hadn't said anything tonight, but he'd certainly made himself clear on other occasions.

She withdrew her hand from his. She refused to play games like these. "I didn't mean that we—"

The grin grew broader; by this time, it had begun to annoy her. She opened her mouth to tell him to forget it—just forget the whole thing.

The comment that came out was on a different track completely. "Dammit, Luke. You sit there looking at me with fire in your eyes, what am I supposed to think? We *are* headed in the same direction, aren't we?"

For a second, Luke seemed surprised by her clear-cut question. Then he recovered. "Oh, yes," he said with a slow smile and a soft laugh. "Yes, we're definitely headed in the same direction. Down the hall and into your bedroom."

Well, that was certainly direct enough. Her lips twitched. And he saw.

Without saying a word, he rose and came around the table. He bent over and simply lifted her, one arm beneath her knees, one across her back. She automatically wrapped her arms around his neck. She was no lightweight, but on his face, so near to hers, there was absolutely no evidence of strain, none.

All at once, Alexandra felt a twinge of misgiving. Or cowardice. He was so tall, so strong. And what did she know about this man, anyway?

Her emotions must have shown clearly. His smile faded; a muscle jumped spasmodically in his jaw. "We can stop right now, Alexandra. But it will be damned hard if we go any further."

The concession was a clear demonstration of his self-control. Her misgivings—if that's what they were—evaporated like smoke on the wind. She touched his face with her fingertips. Then she sighed and laid her cheek on his shoulder.

"I don't want to stop," she said softly. "But I am feeling a bit unsure."

"We're going to take this very slowly, I promise you," Luke said. He moved down the hall toward her bedroom, his footsteps unhurried. When he reached the door, he paused. "Turn on the light."

Her head came up off his shoulder. "Do we have to?"

He looked at her, a half smile quirking his mouth. "I've dreamed of undressing you slowly, of seeing you naked, your hair spread across a pillow. Please."

She was about to tell him that she was thirty-five years old, that she'd had a baby and that she didn't think she chose to be seen. But then he added the last word. Slowly she reached out and flipped the switch.

The bedside lamps came on, casting their soft glow over her yellow comforter-covered bed. But she wasn't looking at the bed. She was looking at the man who held her so effortlessly in his arms.

He walked forward to stand beside the bed and released her legs, letting her toes touch the floor, letting her body come into full, breath-stealing adjustment to his. Her arms remained linked around his neck.

His lips brushed over hers, lightly, teasing, until a soft sound of desire, of passion, erupted from her throat. She slid her fingers into his thick hair and pulled his head down.

His response was electric. His arms tightened and his mouth opened and settled over hers. He thrust his tongue inside with hungry insistence, and she answered his unspoken, intimate challenge willingly. The kiss could have lasted for a moment or much longer, but soon it was not enough for either of them.

His breathing was harsh and irregular when he moved back. His eyes never leaving hers, he sat on the edge of the bed.

She needed no urging to move forward to stand between his thighs. Her khaki skirt buttoned and zipped in the back. He loosened the fastenings, but instead of letting it fall to the floor, he found his way to the hem.

She inhaled sharply when his long fingers leisurely climbed the backs of her thighs, spreading slow heat. When he cupped her bottom in his big hands and squeezed lightly, she thought her poor heart was going to surge right out of her chest. Her knees felt shaky and insecure.

Her head fell back and she closed her eyes, allowing the room to spin crazily. "I think I would like to sit down," she murmured, a touch of anxiety in her voice.

Luke smiled and sat her on his knee. His arm, around her back, his palm flat on her belly, offered support and strength. "Is that better?" he asked tenderly, nibbling at her earlobe, his breath warm.

"Yes." She put her hand on top of his, linking her fingers between his, warmly, affectionately.

One-handed, he turned his attention to the buttons of her blouse, making short work of them. When he parted the sides, though, he made a sound of distress.

She looked at him. "Luke?" His head was down and he was staring at her. She unlinked their fingers and put her hand on his cheek to turn his face toward her. "Is something wrong?" she asked, concerned.

"No, nothing is wrong. Everything is perfect, including you, my beautiful Alexandra." He fisted his fingers in her hair and kissed her, his mouth rough and greedy. Then he stood her on her feet, hastily stripped off her shirt and skirt. She stood before him, clad only in a fragile undergarment.

His hands shook slightly as he touched the delicate straps of her teddy. His smile held a bit of mystery. For a moment, she wondered what had prompted it, then she forgot everything as he peeled the straps off her shoulders, baring her breasts to his avid gaze. The delicate silk and lace followed the rest of her clothes to the floor.

Very gently, very tenderly, as though she were an infinitely precious piece of porcelain, he lifted her. His knee depressed the edge of the mattress as he laid her on the bed. A thin film of perspiration appeared on his forehead.

Alexandra resisted the very real urge to cover herself while his gaze burned a path from her eyes to her toes. "I'm not a girl."

Luke's gaze met hers with understanding. "No, thank heavens, you are not," he said firmly, leaving her with no more doubts, no more concerns, about how she looked to him. "You are a woman, a sexy, provocative, glorious woman." Hands on each side of her head, he leaned down to cover her lips with his.

There was no slow, easy dawdling with his own clothes. Like hers, they were still damp, and his impatience grew, until he finally tore them off and left them in a heap beside the bed.

He was magnificent. His broad chest was hair-roughed and muscular. His hips were slim and his sex was strong and ready for her.

As she was ready for him. She opened her arms and felt the weight of his unclothed body with a swell of desire and recognition that filled her to overflowing. He took the weight of her breast, tasted her. His long fingers tested the dampness between her thighs.

Her own hands were impatient, too. Her nails made trails across the skin of his solid chest until she came to his flat nipples. He groaned as she teased them to hard budding life.

Suddenly, his mouth, his hands were everywhere, tasting, touching, stroking her to a fever pitch. His strong white teeth nipped delicately; his tongue painted her sensitive places with warm moisture. He stoked the fires within her until she thought she would be consumed.

"Luke! Please..." She arched her back with the whispered demand. Her thighs were lax and ready to part; he found the back of her knee and, with one hand, lifted it, at the same moment, sliding his body into the cradle of her femininity.

"Ah, Alexandra, you're so sweet," he breathed. "So..." he caught his breath when she moved "...tight."

His thrusts were slow at first, but her excitement, and the fires within them both, built quickly and would not be denied. She soared wildly, pressing his spine with both hands to bring him even deeper.

"Allie, oh, Allie—"

Luke's hoarse cry signaled the climax that came quickly, simultaneously for them both. They rocketed to another universe, where stars exploded and bodies were reduced to convulsive energy.

When they finally returned to something resembling reality, when their breathing was fairly regular, he asked, "Are you all right?"

Alexandra lay sprawled on her back. Luke had moved just enough so he wouldn't crush her, but not enough that she felt abandoned.

She felt spent and dewy and altogether wonderful. "I'm fine. I'm fabulous, as a matter of fact."

"Where are you going?" he asked, folding his hands under his head and enjoying the view.

Alexandra had on a short, white silk kimono. She'd lost the belt. It was interesting to watch her try to hold it together while she gathered up their clothes. "I'm going to put our clothes in the dryer before they grow mildew," she told him.

"Problem is, I don't have any other clothes here."

"And you wouldn't want to have to go all the way home on a rainy day like this."

"I wouldn't have anything to wear home. Don't forget this." He leaned off the side of the bed and picked up her purple teddy from the floor. Holding it by one strap, he twirled it over his head, grinning the whole time.

She snatched it off his finger. "Thanks." She eyed him measuringly. "I could probably improvise something with a few beach towels."

He gave her a hurt look.

"Or you could just stay in bed until your clothes are dry."

"Now, that sounds like a winner." He settled back against the pillows again, linking his fingers under his head. "Will you bring me breakfast in bed?"

"Don't push it, buster."

"What is it? Are you having regrets?"

She turned her head on the pillow and smiled softly. Their breakfast tray lay on the floor. Luke had convinced her to come back to bed.

For Alexandra, who had been without sex for four years, it had not taken a lot to convince her. The experience last night had been overwhelming. The experience this morning was spectacular. Daniel had been a pleasurable lover, but Luke...she shook her head. She hadn't known some of those things were possible.

"I didn't know you were aware. No, no regrets."

He turned on his back and pulled her beneath his arm. She wiggled a bit, settling herself with her hand on his broad chest.

"What, then?" he persisted. "You were wearing a pensive expression."

"I was just thinking that last night—no, all of yesterday—was a wonderful intermission. But today I have to get back to worrying."

"About David?"

"About him, about the threats, the danger. Sometimes I feel like I've lost control of my life." Her hand made a restless movement across his chest.

He covered it with his own. "Ah-h, your love of independence. You like to do all your worrying by yourself, with no need for someone else."

She was still for a heartbeat. "Maggie's been talking," she said flatly. She would have pulled away, but he held her to his side.

"Maggie and I have been friends for a long time. She saw that I was becoming involved. She didn't want to see me hurt. That was all."

Involved? she thought. How involved was he? This time she succeeded in freeing herself. She pulled the sheet over her breasts and sat up with her arms wrapped around her knees. "Involvement means dependency," she said testily.

"Not necessarily."

"Yes, it does," she insisted, staring at the opposite wall, the blank television screen. "And I will not allow myself to be vulnerable like I was four years ago.

"Look at me now. I've lost control of my life. My son has had to go somewhere else to be safe. I can't get into a car without another car following me. Everything is off track. It's...unsettling."

"Are you saying I took advantage of that?" he asked mildly.

She looked over her shoulder at him and almost melted at the sight. His hair was in disarray and he sported the beginnings of a beard. His tanned skin was dark against her white sheets. He lay with one muscular arm bent, his hand under his head.

He gave her a thin smile.

"That wasn't what I mean, Luke." But was it really? She faced the fact that she was growing dependent on this man, and not only for her physical safety. After last night, she knew was also growing to depend—she wouldn't let herself use the word *need*—on him for emotional support. And she'd taken him to task because she'd been worried about David growing dependent, when the risk was really to her.

Last night was fantastic, glorious, extraordinary. It had awakened feelings in her that she'd thought were long-defunct.

Last night was something she hadn't planned on.

She rested her forehead on her bent knees. "I want to be able to make you understand. Four years ago, I suddenly became chief foreman, overseer, supervisor of a family. Me alone. It scared the hell out of me."

Suddenly, his understanding seemed the most important thing in the world to her. She straightened her spine, turned and faced him, sitting cross-legged. The sheet started to slip and she reanchored it firmly across her breasts. "Would it bother you to talk about Daniel?"

He seemed genuinely surprised. "No. Why should it? He was a big part of your life."

"Then let me tell you about him. Maybe it will help you understand why I am so stubborn about this.

"Daniel was a leader. People respected him because he was also honorable and conscientious. But living with him was difficult in many ways. Don't get me wrong, I loved him. I loved him very much. He was a wonderful husband." She took a deep breath and went on, "He was older than I by several years. And he was always sure that he knew what was best for me."

Luke was beginning to see the emerging picture here. He'd known men like that, strong men who—he broke off the thought as he recalled the day David left to go to West's parents' house.

He had been the one to take charge when the boy argued with his mother, he remembered with a real pang of regret. He'd been the one who knew what was best. He'd decided how the argument would end. He remembered, too, the expression, blank of emotion, on her face that day. Damn! He *hadn't* understood.

"Follow my orders. Do as I say and don't ask questions?" he offered.

She smiled a half smile. "Not quite that bad, but almost. At first, I didn't mind. As a young wife, I got used to it.

"But when he died so unexpectedly, I discovered the many complicated things that make up a life-style, things I should have known and been prepared for, questions I should have asked." Like the fact that the mortgage payment on their beautiful new house was too high for her to manage alone.

She sighed and plucked at a loose thread on the comforter. "Daniel left some insurance, enough to live on while I established my business. I've just gotten myself on solid footing, Luke. I have David's college tuition to look forward to and plan for. Although, if he continues to do as well as he has, I hope he'll get a scholarship. I wasn't planning on getting involved with anyone."

Suddenly, he sat up, too, and wrapped his arms around his knees. "I hadn't planned on it, either, Alexandra. But it happened and I won't run from the idea of..." He broke off. The idea of what? Commitment. Marriage. In his exasperation, Luke was about to reveal more of his emotions than he aimed to.

He had known a lot of women, but not many he would be willing to trust wholeheartedly enough to share his life. Only four, in fact. He'd learned his lesson with his mother by the time he was five. His sister was dead. Maggie was the third.

He still wanted the fourth, of course. He wanted her quite desperately. But he was no longer sure he could afford the emotional price.

He looked over his shoulder. She still sat crosslegged, with the sheet across her breasts. Her gorgeous hair spilled across the smooth, flawless skin of her shoulders; her lips were slightly swollen from his kisses, and red—beautifully, deliciously red.

Maggie was right. Their aims were very different. She could cause him a great deal of heartache. He should move back into David's room until the FBI caught the men they were looking for.

He leaned back on one elbow, ignoring his own warning, and let a smile form on his mouth. He slid a hand under the sheet until he came in contact with a foot, a calf, a soft thigh.

"Luke? What are you doing?" She shimmied. "Oh!"

"What does it feel like I'm doing?" he inquired smoothly, his eyes falling to the sheet over her breasts. He tugged and it came away.

"Our clothes...I don't...ah..."

Chapter 10

"Mom? This is David."

Alexandra smiled to hear her son's voice, glad that they could, at least, talk several times a day. "Hey, honey. How was school today? Did you get all your homework finished?"

"Yes, ma'am. Guess what, Mom? The Chadwicks have a swimming pool indoors. I just noticed it today. This place is big."

"How wonderful," she said weakly. He just noticed something as big as a swimming pool? "But you didn't take your bathing suit, did you?"

"They have extras."

"David, you are behaving yourself, aren't you? Being helpful and not causing the Chadwicks any trouble? Remember, they are older."

"Mo-om. She plays tennis every day on their courts behind the house, and he ran in last year's Peachtree Road Race."

"Oh." She tried—and failed—to picture West's parents. "Well, don't forget to make your bed and hang up your clothes."

"The Chadwicks have servants to do all that," he said carelessly.

Alexandra was struck dumb for a minute. When she spoke again, there was more than a hint of asperity in her voice. "Do it, anyway. I wouldn't want you to get out of the habit."

"Yes, ma'am," said David wearily. "How much longer do I get to stay here?"

She could have wished for a better-worded question. "I'm not sure, honey. It shouldn't be much longer."

"No problem, Mom," David said. "As long as you're okay," he added hastily, almost as an afterthought. "Is Luke there with you?"

She looked at the man lounging comfortably on her sofa. The sunlight was streaming in over his shoulder.

He had gone home to shave and shower and change clothes. He was dressed in khaki pants and another blue dress shirt. He was reading the evening paper, his feet, in leather-tasseled loafers, crossed on an ottoman.

To an outsider, the scene would have appeared quite warm and domestic. She shook off the feeling of awareness that accompanied the thought. "I'm fine, honey, and Luke is here. Would you like to speak to him?"

Luke rose and encircled her waist with his arm as he took the telephone from her. "How are you doing, sport?" Alexandra heard the conversation, but only as background. Servants? Plural? She sighed.

"She really is fine, David. I hope this mess will be straightened out soon so you can come home." He paused. "Here she is." He handed the phone back to her. "He's in a hurry."

"Everything's okay, then, Mom? I'll call you tomorrow. Miss you. Bye."

"Miss you, too. Bye, honey."

She let her hand rest on the receiver for a minute.

"He seems to be all right," Luke commented.

"He's having a ball," she answered wryly. "The Chadwicks have an indoor pool and servants to pick up after him. I hope he'll be able to readjust to real life when this is all over."

Luke chuckled under his breath as he folded the paper and laid it aside. "I can understand how he would enjoy being in a house again."

Alexandra paused on her way to a chair. "What's that supposed to mean?"

Luke shrugged in an attempt to dismiss the subject. "Nothing important."

But Alexandra wasn't about to let him get away without explaining. She waited, watching him patiently. Finally, he said, "David doesn't like condo living."

"How do you know?"

"I can tell. That's why he's so interested in the house I'm building."

Her knees suddenly felt weak. She sank into the chair. "He's never complained to me." She wished she hadn't sounded so defensive, but she was surprised at the depth of her feelings. David had, in some small way, betrayed her and it hurt.

Why would he talk to Luke and not to her? She had watched as man and boy grew close. Though it was temporary, she had even been grateful for the masculine influence in David's life. But now she was angry with herself for not having recognized her son's feelings.

Abruptly she rose from her chair and headed in the direction of the hallway, not knowing why, or where, she was going, only knowing that she suddenly needed to be alone.

"Alexandra, I'm not going to let you run away." He suited his actions to his words, catching her waist as she walked past him.

"I'm not running."

He pulled her off balance, and she lost her footing, landing on his lap. He wrapped his arms around her and held on firmly.

"Let me go, Luke."

"Not until we finish this discussion."

"We're finished."

"We've barely started." He tenderly brushed feathers of hair away from her face and cradled her head on his shoulder. "I am not going to let you feel guilty."

She wouldn't deny that she felt guilt, but she looked up at him, peeved. He was getting to be darned good at knowing what she felt.

His smile was slightly twisted. "Your face is easy to read. David, more than anyone, appreciates how you have coped since your husband died. Alexandra, he wasn't complaining when he talked to me. He's so proud of you that he beams with it. He told me the whole story of how you got your career off the ground, how hard you work, all the famous people you've done special caricatures for."

She felt tears burn against the back of her eyes. She fought them and kept the firmness in her voice. "Then why do you think he's unhappy?"

"Not unhappy. Don't misunderstand—that wasn't what I said. But he's made a few statements that I found revealing."

"Like what?"

"Let me see if I can remember." Luke thought for a minute. "You've been to the house. He liked the big garage because it has a place for the race car and plenty of room to tinker. He was impressed with the fact that it can't be seen from any of the neighbors' houses or from the road. He liked the idea of privacy, he said."

Actually, the boy had said that he couldn't remember how it felt to go out to toss a ball or just lie in the grass without feeling self-conscious about some grown-up watching. But he wasn't going to tell Alexandra that. "He wondered if I was going to buy a dog, or put up a basketball goalpost in the driveway."

"I'm sorry he didn't feel comfortable enough with me to talk about this." She heard the frailty creep into her tone and she *hated* it. "Please, let me get up. I'm uncomfortable."

He let her go and she immediately began to pace, but she didn't run away. "Sweetheart, a boy naturally wants a house with a yard large enough for a dog to run in. Do you realize how much David wants a dog?"

She stopped dead still in the middle of the room, her hands on her hips. As he watched, she seemed to go someplace else. "I had a house I loved. It was my dream house."

Luke sat forward, suddenly attentive, not to what she said but to her demeanor. Something was wrong with her, he noticed in alarm. A deep, gut-wrenching fear that appeared in her green eyes, turning them dark. He'd seen a lot of emotions cross her face, but he had never seen fear. What the hell had caused it?

"I worked on the plans with an architect for a year. It was beautiful." Her voice broke on the last.

Her words were coming out in stop-and-go jerks; her voice climbed with a touch of hysteria. He started to rise, but she gestured for him to stay where he was. She took a breath and quickly had the hysteria under control. But the fear remained, and anger joined it. "I couldn't keep the house. Okay?"

Luke waited, wanting to help, wanting to do something, anything. Her heart swelled with sadness as he witnessed her pain. He took a breath and blew it out through pursed lips. "Sweetheart, I'm so sorry..."

She didn't even hear him. She was preoccupied, profoundly upset. He could have kicked himself. She certainly didn't need anything else to upset her right now.

He stood up and came to her, but he didn't touch her. He would be there, but he wouldn't interfere, not unless she needed him.

"I lost my house because I couldn't pay the bills. Not only couldn't I pay the mortgage, I couldn't pay the gardener, or the pool man, or the electric bill, or a hundred other bills that go along with a house."

"And you had no one," he said heavily.

The statement didn't require a comment. She took a deep shuddering breath and crossed her arms before she faced him squarely. He was relieved to see that most of the fear had faded from her gaze, but a trace of it still lingered.

"I can afford the condo, Luke. Me." She jabbed herself in the chest with her thumb. "I can make the payments. I don't have to worry about spending myself into homelessness to keep up a house. David..."

All the fight went out of her. She shook her head and sighed as she sat down in the nearest chair. "He was only ten. I tried to shelter him. Maybe too much. I didn't want him to feel any more insecure than he was already. But maybe I should have explained some of it."

Luke was quiet for a minute. Then he slid his hands into his pockets and leaned a shoulder against the wall. "It isn't too late to let him know."

She looked up. "Do you think I should tell him?"

"Do you remember..." He shook his head once, violently. "That's an absurd thought, of course you remember. I thought I had made you angry the morning you sent David to the Chadwicks'."

He knew from her studied blank look that she remembered vividly. "I know now, from the things you've told me, that you weren't angry as much as threatened. I feel very badly about what I did. I was interfering between you and your son, and I had no right to do that.

"But, sweetheart, I thought I was—no I *was* doing it for David. He needed to be the man in the family. That's a cliché and could be better put, but it tells the story."

He went on as gently as he knew how. He didn't want to hurt her but he suddenly felt it important, perhaps vital, that she understand. "David needed to let you know you weren't alone, that you had him, that he would help take care of you." He looked away from the realization in her eyes. "He needed you to need him."

Alexandra stared at him, feeling sick. Had she, in her bid for independence, in her determination not to need anyone, shut out her own *son?* Failed to understand the wishes of the most important person in her life?

Before she could take the thought further, Luke said, with a bitterness he'd never shown her, "Believe me, I know how it is to be a boy, helpless to support someone you love."

At the sight of his tortured face, her heart went out to him. Her misunderstanding of David's needs could be set aside until she was alone and could analyze it. "Your parents?" she asked softly.

He levered himself away from the wall and went to stand at the window, staring out. But she had seen his features twist into a hard taut mask.

"My father took off when I was a baby. I didn't give a damn about my mother. She was a selfish bitch. The only good thing she ever did was to give birth to Diana, my little sister." He moved his shoulders, as though adjusting a burden. "Diana was an unbelievably sweet child. From her first smile, she was like sunshine in our house. I can still hear her laughter." His voice faded for a minute. When he resumed, it was in a harsher tone. "She was an asthmatic. My mother hated her coughing. Said it got on her nerves.

"I tried to keep her healthy, to take her to the doctor, to make sure she had her medicine... but she got the flu during an epidemic one year. They both did. My mother came down with it first—she died because she was a drunk and undernourished and her body was used up. But Diana's case turned into pneumonia. For a six-year-old child with her condition... she didn't stand a chance."

Alexandra held her fingers to her mouth and blinked back her tears. A child—baby, really. Dear God. "How old were you?"

"Sixteen."

She went to him then and wrapped her arms around him from behind. She laid her cheek against his back and shut her eyes. "You were only two years older than David," she whispered.

He turned and embraced her. "Yeah. That's why I was trying to bring him into the decision-making process. We, the adults in the room, were packing him up and shipping him off without any attention to his fears or his feelings for you. That was why I asked his permission to be responsible for you." He leaned away and smiled at her. "Not because I didn't think you could take care of yourself. You do a damned good job."

She tilted her head back. "But because David needed to be in charge of making one arrangement. Thank you for helping me see that. I will talk to him now about the problems I had after his father's death."

That night, they made love again, softly, tenderly. Alexandra felt closer to him than she ever had to anyone.

Luke thrust his hands through his hair forcefully, as though he could pull out a good idea by the roots. Unfortunately it didn't help.

The feds had picked up the two men, one of them Ned Austin, who had broken into Alexandra's condo and who had tried to snatch David at the racetrack.

Zarcone had come by with the news that the men had been taken at the airport. "We are still trying to get them to open up. No luck so far," he told Alexandra. "But we're sure they are working for someone else. If your son is all right where he is, I'd like you to leave him there for one or two more days."

Alexandra had felt a surge of joy at Zarcone's first words, to be supplanted by another letdown. She wanted David home. Now. She wanted the dirty clothes and the too-loud stereo and the never-ending appetite. She felt like her life, or her control over it, was slipping through her fingers.

She was ready to get things back in order, to come to some kind of decision about her relationship with Luke and to think about her relationship with David.

Luke had given her a lot to think *about*. The thought of the sixteen-year-old boy standing over the graves of his mother and sister still brought tears to her eyes.

"All right," she told Zarcone. "David is enjoying himself immensely. It won't be a hardship for him."

And according to West, his parents were having the time of their lives. "A lot more fun than they ever had with me," he'd added harshly, making her wonder.

After Zarcone had left, she asked Luke about West. "He doesn't seem particularly close to his parents."

Luke shrugged. "I've never met them."

"I need to work for a while tonight," she told him. "I have to get a sketch in the mail tomorrow."

"May I watch?"

She was surprised. "Watch me draw?"

He grinned, eyeing her shorts with a gleam of anticipation. "Yeah."

She hid a smile of response. "Okay, but I have to work. If you distract me, you're out."

"Yes, ma'am."

"What are you working on?"

"Come here and let me show you." When he joined her, she turned on her swivel stool and smiled at him delightedly. For a minute, he was blessed with a glimpse of the woman David had described, the woman with a quirky sense of the absurd, who gave great birthday parties and laughed a lot. "Look."

On the drawing board was a rough sketch of a large shrimp—in white tie and tails, no less. A top hat tilted rakishly on his head and a cane hung from his elbow.

"Well, well," Luke said.

"Do you like him? Is the cane too much?"

"The cane is okay, but I never knew shrimp had elbows."

"My shrimp does. His name is…" She wrote as she spoke and he quickly realized why. "Sheldon de Vaned."

Luke's smile grew into a chuckle, then into a laugh. He lowered his head and planted a soft, warm kiss under her ear. "David was right. You do have a weird sense of humor."

"He's going to be on the new menus at The Shrimp Society." He looked blank and she added, "The restaurant on Piedmont Street."

"I thought that was a club for short people."

Alexandra made a face and punched his arm. "My sense of humor is weird? You're as bad as I am."

"Let's be bad right now," he urged in his low, sexy voice. Wrapping his arms around her beneath her breasts, he pulled her off balance against him.

Later, as they lay together in the afternoon sunlight, she said, "You know, you're very good for me. I didn't think I would be able to laugh or enjoy myself until this was all over. But these past couple of days have been—" She searched for a word. "Fun?"

Luke laughed and rolled her toward him.

It was very late before Alexandra got back to Sheldon.

"I need to run out to the house for a little while. Would you like to go?" Luke asked from the door of Alexandra's studio. "I've cleared it with Zarcone."

Her skirt today was navy blue. With it she wore a blouse the color of her eyes. "I was sort of waiting for David to call," she replied hesitantly.

"I won't be long. West is coming by to work." Luke's worries were beginning to take on enormous proportions. The deadline was fast approaching. He and West had thought that capturing Ned Austin and his cohort would move the FBI forward. But nothing had come of their arrests except that indictments were being prepared for the grand jury.

The FBI had managed to get bail denied; for now, anyway, the men were safe in jail.

"Okay, then." She dropped her charcoal pencil and swiveled her chair. "I'd like to see the progress you've made."

"I like you in skirts," said Luke when he joined her on the deck of his new house an hour later.

She smiled over her shoulder. "Do you?"

"Yeah." He pinned her against the rail. "They show off your long luscious legs," he growled in her ear.

She rested her arms on his. "I hate to disillusion you, but I don't wear them for that reason. I wear them because they're cool."

His head came up. "Speaking of that, is it me or is the breeze off the river cooler today?"

"It's definitely cooler."

"I used to get depressed when summer was over, did you?"

"Yes, but not anymore. Now I breathe a sigh of relief. What did the builder say? The house looks almost done to me."

"A couple of weeks more. They're going to fill the pool tomorrow. And pour the driveway next week."

And then you will be leaving the condo, Alexandra said to herself. They would see him again, she didn't doubt that now. But when he moved away, nothing would ever be quite the same.

"It's a beautiful house, Luke." Determinedly she shook off her blue mood and grinned over her shoulder at him. "I'm glad I won't have to make the mortgage payments on this place. Or pay the electric bill."

He chuckled, but then he sobered.

"I won't have any mortgage payments. I paid for this place outright. Every nail, every block, every brick and rock are mine."

Alexandra was stunned into silence. "I didn't know people did that," she said.

"It isn't the most productive way to tie up your money. But I wanted to own my own home, to know it was mine. And I had the money. I haven't had a lot of time over these past ten years to spend it."

Alexandra was rather intimidated by someone who built a new house for cash. She kept quiet about it, though.

Shortly after they returned from the house, West entered the condo with two briefcases and a sour expression. "That damned retirement dinner is tomorrow night. I'm not ready to lick the floor for Henderson, are you?''

"Hell, no. But we've got bigger worries. The week's deadline is up tomorrow, too. If something's going to happen, it will happen then."

Luke called Zarcone to see if any progress had been made. The FBI man told him that a substantial deposit had been made to Ned Austin's wife's bank account. Now they were trying to trace the corporation, a dummy, of course. They hoped to have an answer by Monday.

Luke hung up and waited until they had closed themselves in the dining room before he repeated the conversation to West.

"Monday will be too late to nab the guy," West said unnecessarily.

Luke worried his lower lip with his thumb and forefinger. "Listen, West, I have an idea. See what you think...."

Chapter 11

The Bolton retirement dinner was to be held downtown at one of Atlanta's oldest and most prestigious clubs. Alexandra had heard of the place but had never been a guest there.

She dressed carefully for the evening in a floor-length gown of white silk. The halter style was classic—thank goodness, for it was several years old. The silk draped gracefully over her breasts, nipped in at the waist and left her shoulders and back bare. She had arranged her hair in a loose French twist. As she slid her feet into silvery sandals, she realized that, if she hadn't been so focused on the perilous situation, she would have enjoyed dressing for a formal party again.

When the doorbell rang, she picked up a small silver bag and a white stole with gossamer silver threads and went to answer.

West, dressed in a tuxedo, stood staring at her for a long minute. "Well, hell," he blurted out. "I shouldn't have given up so quickly."

She smiled. Though West was a flirt, he rarely lost his composure and she was flattered that he'd lost it now. "Thank you. That was a compliment, wasn't it?"

"You look like a Greek goddess."

"Oh, come now. A goddess?" She laughed.

Luke's deep voice rolled out of the hallway behind Alexandra. He had brought his clothes here to dress. "Not a Greek goddess—they're made of marble. Like an exquisitely beautiful, flesh-and-blood woman," he said, his husky tone leaving her breathless.

He joined them at the door. And her eyes went to him immediately. He was magnificent, tall and strong, his broad chest and wide shoulders clearly defined in the black and white of formal evening clothes.

They both missed the wry smile that swept across West's face. "I'm driving," he said. "Shall we go?"

Alexandra felt more than one glance of appraisal as she entered the club between the two good-looking men. She barely had time to scan the elegant lobby before they were greeted by the honoree.

The senior partner was a refined gentleman of obvious dignity. But, having been introduced, Alexandra decided there was no warmth in the man. She didn't like him.

"Lucius, West, good to see you," he said stiffly. Indicating the woman who joined the group, he added offhandedly, "You know my wife?"

"Yes," said West, shaking hands with his boss. "How are you, Mrs. Bolton?"

Luke took over. "Mrs. Bolton, may I present Alexandra Prescott?"

"I'm very happy to meet you," Alexandra acknowledged. "Thank you for having me."

"We're very glad you could be here, my dear," said Mrs. Bolton graciously. Alexandra decided she liked the senior partner's wife a lot better than she liked him.

Mr. Bolton was conspicuously silent.

Others were behind them. "Congratulations, sir," said Luke before they moved on.

West grinned at Luke. "Looks like we're still in the doghouse."

"Champagne?" Luke asked Alexandra as they entered the huge ballroom.

"Yes, please."

Luke got their drinks from the bar while West introduced her to several people. As soon as a conversation was started, however, he would edge her away and head for another group.

Over the course of the next few minutes, she noticed that both men were strangely tense. One or the other of them always had a hand on her arm. They watched her as if they expected her to flee.

"What is the matter with you two?" she asked finally when she'd been dragged off in the middle of another exchange.

"Nothing," answered Luke shortly.

She decided to ignore them and enjoy herself. She looked around. "This is an impressive room." Light from the huge chandeliers sparkled on crystal and silver, diamonds and gold. A string quartet played Mozart softly beneath the hum of well-modulated voices.

"Mr. Henderson, it's nice to see you again," Luke said. His tone was mild, but Alexandra felt the tension in the grip of his fingers on her arm.

The man turned suddenly, his elbow knocking against the champagne flute in her hand. A bit of the golden liquid sloshed over the rim. His eyes were cold as they met those of the two men standing on each side of her.

"I'm so sorry, Mrs. Prescott." His apology lacked sincerity. "I hope I haven't spoiled your gown."

"No harm done."

"I'm glad."

She knew that there was something going on here but she wasn't sure what. She tried to smooth the moment with a casual comment. "I hope you don't think I was rude the day we ran into each other at the airport, Mr. Henderson. I was anxious to see my son."

He turned that cold gaze on her. She was chilled, so unnerved, that she took a step backward.

"I don't know what you're talking about. I haven't been to the airport in months. Now, if you'll excuse me," he said abruptly.

"What in the world..." She turned to West. "You remember me telling you about seeing your client at the airport? Why would I make up something like that?"

Her gaze swung back to watch, puzzled. The man was almost running. Or would have been if the room hadn't been so crowded. He was halted by a buxom woman in a wheelchair, who reached out to grasp his sleeve. He tried to pull his arm, his hand away.

At that moment, he turned to glance back at Alexandra.

She heard Luke inhale sharply. Suddenly, she became still, frowning.

A similar picture burned in her mind. A man in a uniform. Someone—a child—reaching up for his sleeve. A ring.

The ring she had drawn was unique—she had thought so at the time—and it was the same as the one Henderson wore now. "Is Mr. Henderson a pilot?" she asked, confused by the images racing across her mind. Her eyes sought Luke's.

"No, he isn't." He was watching her, keenly, silently. As though he was waiting for her to reveal...she caught and held her breath. She was so confused.

Slowly, she let out the breath she was holding. Her head swung to West. With dawning suspicion, she realized that he, too, was waiting. "You both know something that I don't. You brought me to this dinner...why *did* you bring me? What is going on?" she demanded.

"Let's get the hell out of here," said Luke.

"We can't," cautioned West. "Not unless we want to be canned on Monday."

"What is going on?" Alexandra asked again.

"The hell we can't," Luke said through clenched teeth. "You stay, then. I'll take Alexandra home."

Both men had ignored her question, as though she hadn't even asked it. All at once, her confusion dissipated and was replaced by indignation. She had a feeling she'd been used and she didn't like it one bit.

She put her hand in the middle of Luke's chest and pushed. It was a childish maneuver, but it got their attention. "Do not talk about me as though I weren't here," she commanded. "And answer my question."

"Not here," Luke muttered.

"It would be rude to leave so soon after we arrived," Alexandra informed them calmly. She was still holding the champagne glass. Pointedly, she toasted a passerby and sipped. "Besides, I don't want to leave," she said firmly. Her chin came up to a stubborn angle and she glared at Luke. "You invited me here intending to use me in some way. Don't think I don't want answers, but I dressed for this occasion. I'm hungry and I intend to have dinner first."

Luke glowered; West chuckled.

"Shall we find our table?" she said.

The crabmeat cocktail was delicious. The terrapin soup was delicate and divine. The sparkling conversation of their tablemates was amusing. And the steaming beef Wellington had just been set before them when West murmured, "Oh, my God."

He was staring blankly at the Boltons' table.

"What is it?" Luke asked in a low voice.

Clutching his napkin, he stood. "Excuse me. I'll be right back."

They watched him wend his way through the sea of circular tables until he reached the one where the honoree was holding court. He spoke to an older couple, nodded to Henderson and Bolton, and then turned right around and headed back.

He dropped his napkin on the table. "Luke, call Zarcone. Come on, Alexandra. I'll get the car." He turned to the others at the table. "Please forgive us. A small emergency," he said with his engaging grin.

The grin survived only until they got out of the room.

"West, what happened?" asked Alexandra. "You are as white as my dress."

"I happened to see my parents at the table with Bolton. I just don't like the idea that they've left David home alone. I want to check on him."

Luke almost stumbled when he heard West's statement. He had to admit that West made a valiant effort at improvisation. Hell and damnation to that bastard, Henderson.

Had the Chadwicks let the information slip about the youngster who was their houseguest? Of course they had. Casual dinner conversation. If not, the three of them wouldn't be rushing over there right now.

"Good idea," he said. "You're going for the car? I'll stop and call Zarcone. Meet you out front."

Alexandra had also paled. "David's in some kind of danger, isn't he?" She looked from one of the men to the other. "Oh, God, hurry up."

Lights were blazing at the Chadwicks' West Paces Ferry mansion when they drove up. West pulled into a circular driveway and stopped at the front door. Zarcone screeched in right behind them with three other men. They all piled out of the cars. Zarcone deployed his men to the sides of the house and ran to the front door with West, Alexandra and Luke.

"Damn," said West. "I don't have my key." He jabbed the button and they heard ponderous chimes inside. He jabbed again.

The door was opened by a middle-aged man. "Mr. West, how...er...nice..." His voice trailed off in the wake of the four people who pushed him aside.

"Where's the boy?" demanded West.

"Master David? I believe he's swimming, sir."

At that moment, David came in from the back of the hallway, wearing bathing trunks and beach shoes, a damp towel slung around his neck. He smiled. "Hi, Mom. Hi, Luke, Mr. Chadwick."

"David," cried Alexandra. She raced to hug him. True to form, David endured it for a minute. Then he began to wiggle.

"What's up, Mr. Zarcone?"

"To tell you the truth, David, I'm a little confused, myself." He turned to West. "I'll leave some extra men here through tomorrow. Two on the grounds and one inside." He let his gaze roam over the three-story entrance hall where they were standing. "Tough duty. They ought to get hazard pay."

"Luke, don't you think you and West should explain yourselves now, while Mr. Zarcone is here to hear the story?"

"No, not here," Luke said without hesitation. "Zarcone can come back with us to the condo." He fixed the shorter man with a scowl. "You can come, but you have to be quiet and let us handle things."

Zarcone sputtered. "Take it or leave it," West added.

"I'll take it," Zarcone said sourly. "But I'll give you fifteen minutes' head start before I get there. Then, unless you give me a damned good reason not to, I'm butting in."

When West pulled into his parking slot and turned off the engine, both of his passengers were silent, as they had been during the entire drive home.

Alexandra, wedged into the middle of the front seat between the two men, spoke in an adamant tone that did not allow for argument. "I can't wait to hear this. Ten minutes."

Luke almost smiled at the tough wording of the command. She waited. Finally, he heaved a sigh and got out. She slid across the seat. Ignoring the men, she marched to her door.

West joined Luke on the sidewalk.

"Damn, she's pigheaded," Luke said.

West gave a nod of agreement. "But she's still the only one who can solve this problem. Don't you think one of us should—"

"Yeah," said Luke, suddenly realizing that she was about to walk unescorted into an empty house. He sprinted to catch up with her. He followed her inside, switching on lights as he went, and made a quick but thorough search of the rooms.

Alexandra was waiting for him in the living room. "Are you going to your place to change?"

He yanked at the bow tie. "No, I'll be right here."

"Then if you will excuse me, I'll be back in a minute," she said, still cool. She looked over her shoulder one last time as she left the room.

He couldn't read her expression, but he was fully aware of the sleek, smooth skin of her back. His memory of how it felt under his hands was vivid and stimulating.

"All right. Let's have it," said Alexandra when they were all seated in her living room.

West nodded at Luke as though to say, "You take the lead." Luke gave him a wry grin. Then he leaned forward in his chair, resting his forearms on his knees. He looked down at his clasped hands for a brief minute. "It might be better if you begin."

"Better for whom?" she snapped.

"For all of us. Please, Alexandra, tell us what you saw."

"All right." She surged to her feet, plunging her hands into her jeans pockets, and walked away from him and West. "First, I saw Mr. Henderson at the airport. He was dressed in a warm-up suit. Navy blue, I think. He sat beside me and chatted for a while." She scuffed the carpet with the toe of her sneaker. "Then I saw him tonight at the party and he told me he had not *been* at the airport. Obviously I am delusional.

"But then . . ." She walked to the mantel, running her fingertips along the edge of the wood. "I think you should call Zarcone," she finished softly.

"Not yet," said Luke urgently. "Go on, finish it."

"I can't. I need my sketch pad. Zarcone brought it back and I can't remember where I put it."

"You don't need your drawing. You are an artist, trained to observe," he said roughly. "You know what you saw, Alexandra. Just describe it for us."

Her eyes reflected the hurt brought on by his harsh words. He knew that she couldn't bear being given orders to without explanation. Her husband had demanded she obey because he said to. "Why? Why are you doing this? I don't understand any of it."

"Dammit, can't you just trust me?" He slapped the arm of his chair. The sharp sound made Alexandra start.

West stepped in at that point. "Cool it, Luke," he warned. He turned to Alexandra. "Alexandra, you will get an explanation, I promise. But for now it's very important that you tell us what you saw without any prompting."

She placed her hands on her hips and drummed her fingers on the denim. "I saw a woman reach for Mr. Henderson's sleeve. It reminded me of a drawing I had done in the airport. A child reaching for the sleeve of a man in a pilot's uniform." The statements came out staccato, in perfect rhythm with her anger. "The man in the airport tried to pull away. He was wearing a distinctive ring that looked like Mr. Henderson's."

She heard the audible sighs that escaped them both at her last words. "What?"

Luke chose his words carefully. "So you can definitely place him at the airport that day?"

"Of course." She looked from one man to the other. "Does that help?"

"I sure as hell hope so." He relaxed visibly, stretching his long arms along the back of the sofa. "Okay, now we're ready for Zarcone."

"Hold on," said Alexandra. "I thought I was going to get an explanation."

"After you tell your story to Zarcone," said Luke. He came to stand beside her, and turned her to him. His smile was crooked. "Sweetheart, please."

Alexandra twisted away from him. She crossed her arms over her stomach in an attempt to ease the ache there. "Tell me something, Luke. Did you and West see the ring in my sketches? Did you recognize it?"

The two men looked at each other. Neither spoke.

"I thought so. Naive as I am, you know, I never asked myself why you were taking such an interest in my safety. I'm going to make coffee." She left them there and went to the kitchen. As she filled the coffeemaker, she could hear their subdued voices but couldn't make out the words. The ache was quickly becoming a terrible pain.

Instead of returning to the living room, Alexandra went to her darkened bedroom. She sat on the edge of her bed for a few minutes, then with a soft cry she fell backward.

She still didn't understand why, but clearly Luke and West had known more than they were willing to tell the authorities. They both seemed determined that she should be the one to figure it out, to steer her toward the facts rather than simply reveal what they knew.

She turned her head restlessly against the spread, trying not to remember the glorious lovemaking that had happened here. She had thought she was falling in love, that she might, after four lonely years, be ready to give her heart again.

But he was not the person she'd thought he was. She squeezed her eyes shut. She could hardly believe that he had deceived her.

He knew her vow—never again would she allow a man to dominate her life. She would only accept a partner, not a guide, not a manager, not a protector.

Now, her disappointment was deeper and darker than any emotion she'd ever felt.

He was there, standing in the door to her room looking at her. He had not made a sound and her eyes were still closed but she knew he was there. With a silent groan, she rolled away, to the side, drawing her legs up, curving her back. When she tried to see ahead, her future looked so black.

"Alexandra, sweetheart." He crossed the floor and sat beside her. The mattress dipped with his weight. She held herself against the urge to roll toward him. "Please listen to me."

"I don't think so."

Luke felt his heart twist painfully. He hated seeing her like this. She was always so straight and confident. "Alexandra...I know you don't understand this, but West and I have been deeply troubled over something." He paused. "We were trying to handle an impossible situation in the only way we could think of, and we used you to do it," he said in a low voice. "I obviously didn't realize how it would appear to you. But, I promise you, I would never knowingly hurt you. Or David. Never. I care about you both too much."

He finally succumbed to the temptation to touch her, but she stiffened when she felt his hand on her back. He withdrew immediately.

The doorbell rang. "There's Zarcone. I know this is hard for you—"

He broke off when she swung her legs off the bed and stood up. "Would you please tell him I'll be out in a minute?" she asked as she headed for the bathroom.

"Sure." Luke continued to sit for a moment, feeling tired and depressed. What else could they have done?

At last, he stood and went to join West and Zarcone.

The story didn't take long to tell. Zarcone was silent through most of it, interrupting only once or twice to clarify a point. When Alexandra finished, she felt drained. "I'm not certain what the value is of this information. Maybe they—" she waved at the two men, having avoided looking at them until now "— will tell *you*. They haven't told me anything." She heard her own bitterness come through, and she felt a moment's guilt. But only a moment.

Zarcone looked at her sympathetically. "I think I understand." He turned to the two men. "This man, Henderson, is a client of the firm you work for, isn't he?" he asked Luke.

"We were assigned to handle his business," Luke answered guardedly. He shot a look at West.

"So he's *your* client. And you can't tell me what that business is?"

Luke shifted uncomfortably in his chair. "No. The lawyer-client confidentiality rule—"

"What?" Alexandra barked. "My son was almost kidnapped and you didn't say anything because of some stupid rule?"

"Wait." Zarcone held up his hand. He got to his feet and began to pace. "There is a connection between this man that Mrs. Prescott saw at the airport, the threats, the break-in, the murder." He paused. "And the fact that this man was in a pilot's uniform."

"Make them tell you," Alexandra said.

"Mrs. Prescott, I know how you feel. But lawyer-client confidentiality is one of the bedrocks of our legal system. The reasons may not seem logical to someone who isn't a member of the bar." He spread his hands. "But I am."

"Oh, great," said Alexandra. "I'm surrounded by lawyers."

Zarcone and West left together. Luke joined them on the porch for a few last words.

"I appreciate what both of you have done. It wasn't easy to walk such a fine line."

"No," said Luke. "What I'm about to say may put me on the other side of that line, but I'm going to say it, anyway."

"Luke," West warned.

"You might want to go inside," Luke told him. "There is no reason for both of us to take the chance."

"Hell, Luke, what kind of man do you think I am? Whatever happens, we're both responsible."

Luke had always known that West Chadwick had a keen mind. Now he also knew that West was no light-weight when it came to loyalty. He would be a valiant friend, one to be depended on when times got tough. He nodded and turned to Zarcone. "Don't let any grass grow under your feet. Time may be important."

"You mean he may be planning to leave town?" Zarcone asked. Then he waved away his own question. "You're not going to answer that. I'm on my way." He hurried across the lawn to his car.

Luke's hand was on Alexandra's door, when West spoke. "Good luck. She's pretty mad but she's smart. She'll understand and come around."

Luke couldn't hide his surprise.

"Hey, I've got eyes," West went on. "If I couldn't have her, you'd be my next choice. Besides, she's the kind of woman who needs a ring on her finger. I'm not sure I'll ever be ready for that."

Luke went inside. Alexandra was waiting for him, fire in her eyes. "You needn't stay tonight, Luke. I doubt that I would be considered bait any longer."

He slid his hands into his pockets and looked at her. "You never know."

She seemed to hesitate for a minute. Then she said, "Good night, then."

"Good night, sweetheart."

"Don't call me that," she snapped.

She almost made it to the door before the phone rang. The sound halted her in her tracks, and she turned back to Luke, fear and despair in her eyes. "Oh, no," she whispered.

"I'll get this one," he said.

"No." She held up her hand. "No, I'll get it." She went swiftly to the phone, but before she answered, she sank into a chair and took a deep breath.

Luke's fists were clenched as he watched and admired her strength. God, if he could only spare her.

"Hello." The color left her face as she listened. Her delicate frame swayed slightly.

It was all he needed. He was across the room in two steps. He grabbed the phone from her and shouted, "Listen, you damned son of a bitch..." His voice trailed off when he realized he was cursing a dial tone.

"Same old, same old. He said what he had to say and hung up."

"He won't be saying it much longer," Luke said with determination.

She tried to stand but didn't make it. Luke scooped her up in his arms and held her close to his heart as he headed for her room.

He laid her on the bed and went to the bathroom for a cold cloth. This he laid on her head.

"Sweetheart, can't you even look at me?"

"Maybe I'll be able to later. Not now. Please, just leave me alone."

Late that night, Zarcone rang Luke's doorbell. West was there.

"I was hoping I would catch you together," he said. "I thought you would want to know that when we pieced the story together and forced it on Ned Austin, he caved."

"That's great, Zarcone," said Luke, as if he didn't care one way or the other.

"It seems that the pilot, Brigadol, was arranging shipments of chips for Mr. Henderson. Unfortunately for him, he got greedy. He decided to hold off on one delivery. Henderson killed him, we don't know where yet. Not where he was found, that's for sure.

"Then he put on the uniform in order to gain access to Brigadol's locker. Places like that are normally restricted to the public. Not just anybody can go walking in there. He got the chips out of the locker. Changed back into his clothes and that's when he ran into Mrs. Prescott.

"Her sketch of Henderson—or his ring—was the only connection between him and the pilot or the smuggling ring. We'd been watching the pilot—not seriously, but keeping an eye on him. While her drawing wouldn't serve as evidence, her eyewitness to his presence would. Don't know why he lied. Maybe he thought he was such a big wheel anyone would believe him over her. Don't know where he got such a stupid idea as that, either."

Neither of them responded for a minute. Then West said, "Thanks, Mr. Zarcone. We really appreciate all you've done."

"All in a day's work, boys. See you later."

"Yeah," Luke said. "See you."

Chapter 12

"She won't *listen* to me," Luke raged, pacing West's living room.

"And you won't apologize to her." West shook his head in obvious disgust. "You're as stubborn as two mules in a tug-of-war."

"How can I apologize for doing my job? An apology means you won't do it again, doesn't it? And I would have to do the same thing, the ethical thing, under the same circumstances."

West shrugged. "So, smart man, where does the ethical thing leave you when your bed is empty on a cold winter's night?" He paused. "You *were* going to ask Alexandra to marry you, weren't you?"

"Hell, yes." Luke was quiet for a minute. "David's on my side."

West laughed without humor. "David's always been on your side," he said wryly. "But he's not going to dictate her decision."

Luke slumped into a chair and buried his face in his hands. "I know," he said quietly, feeling his energy dissolve like sugar in hot tea.

He sat that way for a minute, then he straightened. "If she won't even try to understand my position, if she won't listen, then maybe she isn't the woman for me."

"Maybe not," he agreed with ambiguous amiability. "Maybe you have to face the fact that Alexandra isn't the princess to reign in that castle you're building out on the river. Maybe you're just going to have to start looking again."

That brought Luke's head around. "It isn't a castle."

"Damned close."

"And don't get any ideas," he warned. "She's not the woman for you, either. If you even look at her sideways, I'll—"

West threw back his head and roared with laughter.

An hour later, David entered his mother's studio. He wandered around for a minute. Then he blurted out, "I think you should apologize to Luke."

She looked up from the drawing board. "Oh, you do, do you?"

She was wary. David had been very angry with her, refusing even to discuss the situation for a whole day. The response was so unlike him that she had pulled back. Her relationship with her son was on shaky ground right now and she didn't want to take any chances.

He crossed the room and perched on a swivel stool. The sunlight coming through the window behind him threw his face into shadow. For the first time, she noticed that his childish features—his jaw, his nose, his forehead—were beginning to sharpen and define themselves into a manly cast.

Backlit as he was, a barely perceptible fuzz was visible on his cheek and chin. Her boy was growing up. She had already noted that his voice was more often baritone than alto these days. Now, it seemed it would soon be time for him to shave.

"Yes, ma'am," he said, unaware of her observations. "I think Luke loves you, Mom. And I know he's the best thing that's happened to you since Dad died. You thought he should have gone against his sworn oath but aren't you always telling me that a person's word is his bond? Didn't you say that a good reputation is more valuable than gold? And—"

"Enough, enough," Alexandra protested. She tried to smile. "I never thought to have all the maxims quoted back to me."

"Well, Luke didn't have a choice, Mom. He's a lawyer and that client-privilege thing is intense."

She tossed her pencil on the board and watched it roll to a stop. Then she raked her hair back with her fingers and gave a heavy sigh. "I know."

"I think he and West are pretty brilliant. To get you to that party, and make you see for yourself what they couldn't tell you."

She lifted her eyebrows. "Oh? So West is included in this admiration society?"

David hunched his shoulders dismissively. "West isn't so bad, I guess. He just wasn't right for you. Luke is. So. Are you going to?"

Alexandra, distracted for a minute, looked at him blankly. "I'm sorry. Am I going to do what?"

"Apologize, Mom."

"I'm going to think about it," she said slowly.

"Mo-om."

"David, I said I'll think about it." Her voice was sharp this time.

He shrugged. "Okay. I guess that's all I can ask."

"You betcha."

He left. A few minutes later, she heard him leave the condo, whistling.

David was right. The moral concept of client confidentiality was inviolate.

She had reacted with her emotions, not letting her brain have a say. She had wanted to punish Luke, feeling that he had put her son's life in danger. But the truth was, he had done everything, short of breaking his oath, facing disbarment, and possibly jail, to ensure that she and David *were* safe.

It was up to her to apologize. And she was scared out of her shoes.

David answered the door of Luke's condo. "Mom, I knew you'd come through," he said. "Now, I've laid the groundwork. Luke is in a very good mood. So all you have to do is ask him to marry you. I think he'll say yes. You should keep your fingers crossed, of course."

"Are you leaving?" she asked when he moved to pass her.

"Mo-om, you don't want me around during this big reconciliation scene."

Alexandra stared after him, feeling as though she were being cast adrift. He turned back and gave her a thumbs-up, then a shooing motion. "Don't worry about me." He grinned and waggled his eyebrows. "And by the way, you look terrific."

"Thank you." She had put on her ecru silk blouse and nubby slacks. She wore a little more makeup than she usually did, and she'd left her hair down, only brushing it until it shone.

"I won't worry about how late you get home. After all, you're just next door."

She nodded and finally smiled. The door was open. She stepped across the threshold. The entrance hall was dark but there were lights in the room beyond.

"Hi," said a voice form the shadows of the kitchen.

Alexandra whirled, startled by the large shape looming out of the darkness. Her hand went to her breast. "Hi," she said.

"I'm sorry if I scared you," he said. He didn't sound sorry. He sounded amused. Dammit, she didn't need to be laughed at tonight. She took a step closer to him.

He was smiling, his strong white teeth in contrast with his tanned skin. And his smile was open and genuine. One dark eyebrow arched provocatively.

Her heart accelerated at the sight of him. This was the Luke she was accustomed to seeing. This was the Luke she loved.

"Would you like to come in?"

His question reminded her that there was a hurdle yet to be vaulted before she could think of love or commitment or any of the things she'd come here hoping for. "Ask him to marry you," David had advised. Did she have the fortitude?

"Yes, if you're not busy." She noted that his tie was loose, his shirt collar loosened. He had discarded his jacket. He had a glass in his hand.

"No, I'm not busy. Would you like a drink?"

"No. I won't take—this won't—"

She broke off the impossible attempt at an explanation and sighed as she led the way into the living room. The return of his formal demeanor didn't make this easy.

When she reached the door, she stopped dead still. Packing boxes were everywhere. She turned, her eyes wide as they met his.

His smile had faded and his eyebrows came together in a frown. He took a swallow from the glass. "The house is finished. I'm moving in this weekend."

"I didn't know," she murmured, wishing she didn't sound so dazed.

"Have a seat." He swept a stack of brown packing paper off the sofa. She sank into the cushions. He sat in a chair.

She sat like a proper child, her hands linked in her lap. "I've come to apologize to you, Luke. I wasn't very perceptive. I realize that you have ethics and standards in your profession and rules that you cannot break under penalty of law.''

She glanced at him to see if her apology was having any effect. He had his hand over the lower part of his face and the gray eyes were very serious as he gave her his complete attention.

''I wish that I had listened when you tried to explain. I was hardheaded. And stupid. And I'm very sorry.'' Her voice was infinitely soft by the time she finished.

Suddenly, she felt tears forming in her eyes. What if she lost? The idea hadn't occurred to her until this very moment. And it was a devastating possibility. How would she exist without this man? She *needed* him.

Her chin came up. The tears burned but she fought their falling. A knot formed in her throat, threatening to choke her. But she was determined not to cry.

He set his glass down and leaned forward with his shoulders rounded and his forearms on his thighs. His large hands hung between his knees. She could only see the top of his head; the thick, rich brown hair looked as though it had been combed many times with his fingers.

''It was a hell of a dilemma, Allie.'' His voice was soft, too.

Her heart gave a bound when he used the affectionate name he only used in moments of extreme emotion. When he was kissing her. When he was inside her. She tightened her grip on her fingers.

''I believe in the law,'' he went on. ''Though not always in the way it's practiced. It is far from perfect, but no one has been able to come up with anything better.

"But I love you and David, too, and I don't think I could bear to live without you."

At his words, her fingertips flew to her lips.

"But if I had broken confidentiality, I could not have lived with myself. I wanted to—"

"Stop. Don't, please..." She rose and went to him. The tears were falling now but she paid no attention to them. "I would never want you to be less than you are, Luke. Your integrity and honesty are part of what makes me love you. You wouldn't be yourself if you betrayed your principles."

She sank to her knees beside him. His head came up, his face inches from hers, and she saw her uncertainty mirrored in his eyes. "Oh, my darling," she breathed. "I do love you so."

His arms crushed her to him; he lifted her onto his lap and buried his mouth in the sweet, soft juncture of her neck and shoulder. His next words were muffled. "I knew that my silence could be dangerous for you. All I could do was try to keep you safe. I despaired that either of you would ever understand."

"David did. He was wiser than I was."

When he lifted his head to look at her, she framed his face between her palms. "But I promise I won't ever doubt you again." She pulled his mouth down to hers. "I need you, Luke."

At last, she thought, warmth flooding through her body from his caresses. At last I am exactly where I want to be, where I should be.

* * *

The clear sunlight shone down on the deck over-looking the river. The railings were festooned with white satin ribbons, which weren't particularly com-plementary to the unseasoned redwood but were to-tally appropriate for a wedding. A crowd of about thirty people milled around, waiting for the cere-mony.

It was mid-October. The trees on the opposite bank of the river were at the peak of their autumn colors.

Alexandra looked out on the scene from the master bedroom where she was dressing. "Oh, Maggie, have you ever seen such a perfect day in your life?"

Maggie, dressed in an azure blue suit and matching shoes, grinned at the bride's exuberance. "It is a per-fect day, honey. And I'm so happy for you and Luke. And David, too, of course."

"You're sure it won't be any trouble for you to have him while we're gone?" She and Luke were flying to Maui for two weeks. The travel agent had pushed the Caribbean as being the most romantic place for a honeymoon, but they had vetoed that idea. "Luke wanted to take David with us, but David wouldn't hear of it. He said he's holding out for Japan and all those electronics."

"Of course we won't mind having him. He can go to school and come home with Morris. I think Morris has even talked him into watching soccer practice. Maybe David will even agree to kick a ball or two and have a surprise for you when you get home.

"I'm only sorry we didn't know about your problems. He could have stayed with us instead of West's parents."

Maggie had her feelings hurt over that. Alexandra had tried to explain that everything had happened too quickly for any logical planning. "I wish he'd stayed with you, too," she said dryly. "He came home spoiled rotten. An indoor pool and his own driver. Indeed."

A knock at the door sent Alexandra's eyes to the clock. "Mom, it's time," David called.

She checked her appearance one last time in the mirror. Her tea-length dress was a soft peach silk chiffon. She wore a small matching pillbox with a scrap of veil, her only concession to the bridal consultant who had rushed through all the plans for this wedding.

Maggie handed her a sheath of Talisman roses tied with a dark green velvet ribbon. "Ready?" she asked.

Alexandra put her palm flat to her stomach. "I think so," she said.

David sat on the top step, waiting. He was to give his mother away. He liked that idea. When she came out of the room, he stood up.

His expression was suddenly vulnerable, childlike, but he was trying so hard to be a man. "Mom, you look beautiful," he said quietly. "I think Dad would hope that you and Luke will be happy."

Clearly, he had practiced what he thought would be the right thing to say. His words brought tears to her eyes. Not tears of grief or regret; this was not the day for those. But tears of joy that Daniel had left her with this marvel of a son. "I am happy, honey. So happy."

She held out her arms and David didn't hesitate to walk into them. Maggie slipped back into the bedroom, leaving them alone for a moment. They held each other.

Luke was going to fill their lives with love and passion and joy and laughter and love. Luke would be her husband and a dad to David.

Finally, Alexandra stepped back and blinked to clear her eyes. "And your daddy would be so proud of the man you've become."

She had taken Luke's advice; she had opened up to David, told him things that she'd never told anyone about the weeks and months following Daniel's death. He had been surprised, and he had responded with a maturity that hadn't surprised her at all.

"Shall we go, madam?" said David, his attempt at humor a demonstrable sign that he was as moved as she.

"Certainly, milord. Maggie? Are you coming?"

Her son escorted her through the small crowd, no more than thirty of their friends, to the music of an organ. Alexandra held her head high; the smile on her face was unfeigned, unpretentious.

Luke's eyes never left her as she and David made their way to where he stood with West and the minister. The minister was dressed in dark robes and held a prayer book in his hands.

A white satin kneeling bench had been placed before the huge rock chimney. It was a lovely setting for a wedding. Alexandra felt that the sunlight through the trees laid a warm blessing upon the scene.

The minister recited the traditional words in a deep, practiced voice, which lost nothing in its sincerity. When he asked, "Who gives this woman?" David answered in a clear voice and started to step back.

But Luke forestalled him. He reached for David's arm and brought him back to the spot between them. "You belong right here," he said firmly.

David grinned. Alexandra looked at Luke with her heart in her eyes. The minister took a moment to regain his composure.

And then it was over. The organist switched from classical to pop, the champagne flowed and the guests stuffed themselves on pâté, caviar and Brie.

Ignoring Luke's glare, West pulled Alexandra into his arms and planted a long kiss on her lips. He had surprised several other lawyers present by serving as Luke's best man. He claimed the dividend of a real kiss as a prerequisite of the job.

"The ceremony was nice," he said. "And blessedly short. I hate those long, drawn-out weddings. They're designed to make bachelors like me extremely nervous."

"Forget any more perks. And get us another glass of champagne," Luke said to West, drawing Alexandra firmly to his side. "We have another toast to drink."

"Ah, yes." He shot a look at Alexandra. "Do you think she's going to kill us?" he asked with a grin.

"No, but we will probably end up killing each other," Luke grumbled.

Alexandra gave her new husband a puzzled smile. "What are you two up to now?"

"We've resigned from the firm. We're going into partnership together. Close your mouth, dear."

Alexandra was fully aware that her new husband was planning to make a change. But West had never said a word. She was stunned and instantly apprehensive. "You and West? But your rivalry—you said yourself you fight all the time."

"We discovered during 'Henderson' that we complement each other pretty well, actually," said Luke. "And since we'll always be on the same side, there shouldn't be a problem."

West returned bearing three glasses of champagne. "Here you go," he said, passing them out. "To us, to new partnerships, new enterprises, new wives."

"Get your own wife," Luke growled. But he joined in the toast.

Then West asked, "Are you ready to give out the wedding presents yet? I'm afraid my Jaguar won't survive for much longer with what's inside."

"David," Luke called. "Stay with your mother, will you, while we get something from West's car."

"Sure, Luke. What's this about, Mom? Can I have a sip of your champagne?"

"I have no idea. No, you *may* not."

Just about everything about this day had been a surprise to Alexandra—and a pleasant one. Her fiancé had insisted she leave it all to him while she finished up the work she had scheduled for the next two weeks. He'd called on Maggie, hired the bridal consultant and made Alexandra an appointment to pick out her dress. And told her not to worry about a thing.

It was a measure of her trust that she did not worry. She was discovering that it was rather nice to have someone to depend on when she had work that had to be done.

As long as it didn't go too far.

She intended to see that it didn't.

She heard a stir among the guests and a gasp from David. She turned.

West came first with a long cardboard cylinder in his hand.

Luke was carrying a large basket with a huge white bow; and trailing behind him, right at his heels, watching anxiously, was the most beautiful golden retriever Alexandra had ever seen.

"This is your wedding present, David," he said with a smile. "Maggie and Morris have already given permission for you to take them to their house until we get back."

David stared, mouth agape, as Luke gently set the basket down. The mother retriever checked immediately to make sure her two offspring were all right. Then she sat back on her haunches and looked up at David, tongue lolling, tail wagging.

David sank to his knees and buried his face in the dog's neck. "Oh," he said. "All three of them?" His voice was hoarse and choked.

Luke hitched his trousers and hunkered down beside the boy. He laid a hand on the dog's head. "All three. The mother's name is Martha, but the others

don't have names yet. I trust you can come up with
something more interesting than Martha.''

"I sort of like Martha," David said, scratching behind the dog's ear. At the sound of her name, the
mother dog wagged her tail and licked David's cheek.
"It's very...motherly." David looked at Luke. His
eyes were wet. "Thank you, Luke."

The guests had gathered close to see the dogs. At the
intimate exchange between the boy and the man, they
moved back.

Alexandra had to hold on to West to stay upright.

When Luke stood up again, she stepped into his
arms. "You are..." She shook her head and raised her
green eyes to his. "Words escape me," she whispered, smiling. "Wonderful is so mild." She wrapped
her arms around her husband's neck and brought him
down for a deep kiss. "I love you."

His arms tightened around her and he returned the
kiss with barely restrained passion. "And I haven't
even given you your wedding present yet," he said
when he lifted his head.

"You do pick the most interesting things. What did
you get for me? A vintage car?"

"Nope."

To her surprise, the answer came from West, not
Luke. He held out the cardboard cylinder he'd been
holding to Luke, who took it.

"Thanks for picking it up for me, partner," he said.
He was grinning like a kid at Christmas.

Alexandra enjoyed a passing perception that a kid
at Christmas was exactly what he was. This generous

loving man had never known what a family of mother, father and children was like.

He'd soon find out, she vowed. He had already given her and David so much. They were going to make up to him for all the lonely years.

He nudged her. "Let's go inside. We need a table for this."

Alexandra led the way, intrigued. She hoped it wasn't anything too extravagant. She had given him monogrammed cuff links and the portrait of herself and David for his desk, which he'd asked for. "Luke, you didn't spend a lot of money, did you?"

He chuckled. "I like the idea of a thrifty wife. Now that we're married, I'm turning over all the accounts to you, my love." Hand at her back, he steered her into the dining room.

The table was from her condo, one of the few pieces of furniture that was in place. The beds were another. They would move the rest of her things when they returned from Hawaii.

"But this is something that is an absolute necessity. You'll see." Her curiosity grew as he worked the plastic end free and tilted the cylinder. A roll of blueprints fell out.

"Luke, we already have a home."

"Yeah, but we've got to add on." He spread out the roll, looking for something to anchor it with.

"Here." She slipped off her shoes. He put them on one end, and they held down the rest of the curling roll with their forearms.

When Alexandra realized what she was looking at, she almost burst into tears herself. Her eyes grew as

big as the proverbial saucers. "A real studio!" she
breathed. "A real, *big* studio!" she amended when she
looked more closely. "It's wonderful, Luke. Tell me,
where does it connect? What's this? Is the whole wall
storage space?" She leaned sideways, touching her
head to his shoulder. "I love it. Just think, no more
working out of a spare bedroom!"

He kissed her forehead, leaned closer to cover her
lips. "I thought eventually, Mrs. Quinlan, we might
have another use for the spare bedrooms."

"Then we'd better get started," said Alexandra,
smiling at him with the shine of hope and anticipation in those emerald eyes.

West Chadwick stood on the deck, watching them
through the glass doors. They were laughing, teasing
each other. He had a feeling that the stodgy but resourceful Lucius Quinlan was gone forever. And that
was no loss.

West was feeling strange today. Empty.

Ah, hell, he was just jealous. "I saw her first," he
said to himself.

"But it didn't get you anywhere, did it?" answered
an officious voice inside him. The voice often spoke to
him, but he always managed to dismiss it.

He shrugged and went to look for the gorgeous gallery owner Alexandra had introduced him to earlier.
What was her name, again?

* * * * *

**Another wonderful year of romance
concludes with**

Christmas Memories

Share in the magic and memories of romance
during the holiday season with this collection of two
full-length contemporary Christmas stories,
by two bestselling authors

**Diana Palmer
Marilyn Pappano**

Available in December at your favorite retail outlet.

Only from ▼ *Silhouette*®

where passion lives.

XMMEM

MONTANA
Mavericks

Stories that capture living and loving
beneath the Big Sky, where legends live
on...and mystery lingers.

This December, explore more MONTANA MAVERICKS with

THE RANCHER TAKES A WIFE
by Jackie Merritt

He'd made up his mind. He'd loved her almost a lifetime
and now he was going to have her, come hell or high
water.

And don't miss a minute of the loving as the passion continues with:

OUTLAW LOVERS
by Pat Warren (January)

WAY OF THE WOLF
by Rebecca Daniels (February)

THE LAW IS NO LADY
by Helen R. Myers (March)
and many more!

Only from *Silhouette®* where passion lives.

Is the future what it's cracked up to be?

This December, discover what commitment
is all about in

GETTING ATTACHED: CJ
by Wendy Corsi Staub

C. J. Clarke was tired of lugging her toothbrush
around town, and she sure didn't believe longtime
boyfriend David Griffin's constant whining about
"not being able to commit." He was with her every
day—and most nights—so what was his problem?
C.J. knew marriage wasn't always what it was cracked
up to be, but when you're in love you're supposed to
end up happily ever after...aren't you?

The ups and downs of life as you know it continue with

GETTING A LIFE: MARISSA
by Kathryn Jensen (January)

GETTING OUT: EMILY
by ArLynn Presser (February)

Get smart. Get into "The Loop"!

HE'S A LOVER...

A FIGHTER...

AND A REAL HEARTBREAKER.

Silhouette Intimate Moments is proud to introduce a new lineup of sensational heroes called **HEARTBREAKERS**—real heavyweights in matters of the heart. They're headstrong, hot-blooded and true heartthrobs. Starting in April 1995, we'll be presenting one HEARTBREAKER each month from some of our hottest authors:

> Nora Roberts
> Dallas Schulze
> Linda Turner—and many more....

So prepare yourselves for these heart-pounding HEARTBREAKERS, coming your way in April 1995—
only in

Now what's going on in

CONARD COUNTY ?

Guilty! That was what everyone thought of Sandy Keller's client, including Texas Ranger—and American Hero—Garrett Hancock. But as he worked with her to determine the truth, loner Garrett found he was changing his mind about a lot of things—especially falling in love.

Rachel Lee's Conard County series continues in January 1995 with A QUESTION OF JUSTICE, IM #613.

INTIMATE MOMENTS®
Silhouette

SILHOUETTE... Where Passion Lives

Don't miss these Silhouette favorites by some of our most distinguished authors! And now you can receive a discount by ordering two or more titles!

SD#05786	QUICKSAND by Jennifer Greene	$2.89	☐
SD#05795	DEREK by Leslie Guccione	$2.99	☐
SD#05818	NOT JUST ANOTHER PERFECT WIFE by Robin Elliott	$2.99	☐
IM#07505	HELL ON WHEELS by Naomi Horton	$3.50	☐
IM#07514	FIRE ON THE MOUNTAIN by Marion Smith Collins	$3.50	☐
IM#07559	KEEPER by Patricia Gardner Evans	$3.50	☐
SSE#09879	LOVING AND GIVING by Gina Ferris	$3.50	☐
SSE#09892	BABY IN THE MIDDLE by Marie Ferrarella	$3.50 U.S. $3.99 CAN.	☐ ☐
SSE#09902	SEDUCED BY INNOCENCE by Lucy Gordon	$3.50 U.S. $3.99 CAN.	☐ ☐
SR#08952	INSTANT FATHER by Lucy Gordon	$2.75	☐
SR#08984	AUNT CONNIE'S WEDDING by Marie Ferrarella	$2.75	☐
SR#08990	JILTED by Joleen Daniels	$2.75	☐

(limited quantities available on certain titles)

AMOUNT	$_____
DEDUCT: 10% DISCOUNT FOR 2+ BOOKS	$_____
POSTAGE & HANDLING	$_____
($1.00 for one book, 50¢ for each additional)	
APPLICABLE TAXES*	$_____
TOTAL PAYABLE	$_____
(check or money order—please do not send cash)	

To order, complete this form and send it, along with a check or money order for the total above, payable to Silhouette Books, to: **In the U.S.:** 3010 Walden Avenue, P.O. Box 9077, Buffalo, NY 14269-9077; **In Canada:** P.O. Box 636, Fort Erie, Ontario, L2A 5X3.

Name:_____

Address: _____ City:_____

State/Prov.:_____ Zip/Postal Code:_____

*New York residents remit applicable sales taxes.
Canadian residents remit applicable GST and provincial taxes.   SBACK-DF

Silhouette®